Other published
by Joseph Gol

Books

The Death of Tinkerbell: The American Theatre in the 20th Century, New York, Syracuse University Press, 1967.

On The Dotted Line: The Anatomy of a Contract, New York, CRC Publishing, 1979.

Olympus on Main Street: A Process for Planning a Community Arts Facility. New York, Syracuse University Press, 1980.

Help! A Guide to Seeking, Selecting and Surviving an Arts Consultant, New York, CRC Publishing, 1983.

In Good Form: Paperwork that Works, Madison, Wisconsin, ACUCAA, 1986.

Pollyanna in the Brier Patch: The Community Arts Movement, New York, Syracuse University Press, 1987.

Plays

"The Butterfly that Blushed," a comic fantasy with music for children, Cody, Wyoming, Pioneer Drama Service, 1954.

"Spinner Boy," a one-act play, New York State Community Theatre Journal, Vol. III, No. 3, June, 1963.

"Johnny Moonbeam and the Silver Arrow," anthologized in *Twenty Plays for Young People*, Anchorage, Kentucky, 1967, and in *Plays Children Love*, New York, Doubleday & Co., 1981.

Animals In My Mailbox

And a bunch of other silly, satiric & testy commentaries
on the quirky, heroic or dumb behavior of human beings

Joseph Golden

*To Sue —
Enjoy! (I hope.)
Joe Golden*

Coastal Villages Press
Beaufort, South Carolina

Tabby Manse

Published by Coastal Villages Press,
a division of Coastal Villages, Inc.,
PO Box 6300, Beaufort, SC 29903,
843-524-0075, fax 843-525-0000,
a publisher of books since 1992.
Visit our web site: www.coastal-villages.com.

Available at special discounts for bulk purchases
and sales promotions from the publisher
and your local bookseller.

Cover by Ad Works

ISBN 1-882943-16-3
Library of Congress Control Number: 2003103996

First Edition
Printed in the United States of America

Dedication

This little volume is dedicated to—who else?—my wife, Lucy. Apart from being my wife, helpmate and friend, her yeoman service as in-house critic and editor helped make this collection possible. A grammatical or literary blooper rarely escaped her patient, critical, proofreading eye. It saved me from the embarrassment of perpetrating awkward and stupid linguistic boners, literary gaffes and bad spelling.

If the stuff in this book is readable, rational, and entertaining, blame her.

Contents

Part Four - Entertainment

Part Five - Business

Part Six - This and That

Preface

When you see Joseph Golden on the street, at the supermarket or a cultural event, you can't help but smile, because he is smiling. The same could be said of his Community Forum columns in *The Beaufort Gazette*. Joe could be likened to the Groucho Marx of the newspaper world. He doesn't see life through rose-colored glasses. He is a writer, which is not to be confused with an author who labors over one work and never produces another.

Over the past four years, Joe has been a steady contributor to *The Gazette*. He is knowledgeable as well as witty. He has a knack for poking fun at human foibles. He takes mundane events and makes them extraordinary.

In sum, Joe has a grasp of life and its vagaries that few people possess. I look forward to his offerings because they present a light-hearted view of life that isn't found in Page One headlines about government, murder, war and other bad news.

Welcome to *Animals In My Mailbox*. You will definitely enjoy.

Jim Cato
Publisher/Editor
The Beaufort Gazette

Introduction

Many people ask me where I get ideas for articles I write.
Well, a few people ask. Maybe a tad or two fewer than a few.
Let's see, three persons inquired in 2000. No, two actually. The third
thought I was Harry ("Two Cents Plain") Golden from Charlotte.
When I told the caller Harry Golden was dead, and that I was in no
way related to him, he snarled "Liar" and hung up. So I really can't
count him.

There were two inquiries in 2001. One of them, I'll confess, was
from my brother-in-law, a published writer himself, who simply
wanted to know how I got away with writing so many short, incomplete sentences. Like this one. I told him that only criminals do long
sentences.

In 2002, nobody asked. I'm obliged to attribute this to the generous
and trusting spirit of *The Beaufort Gazette* readers. They must be sublimely confident that I get ideas *someplace*, that my sources might be
private and privileged, and that, as Southern Gentry, it would be im-
polite to ask. So they don't.

Well, for the legion of uncurious readers out there, I'll divulge my
idea source anyway. If you've read any of my little essays of late,
you've held the source, *The Beaufort Gazette*, of course. No, not the
headline, global calamity stuff. Wars, rebellions, espionage, environmental havoc, terrorism and other international psychoses are the bai-
liwick of the op-ed pontificators on the Editorial Page.

What inspires and captivates me are not the periodic bouts of insan-
ity that afflict global institutions. Rather, it's the vivid and unpredictable kaleidoscope of quirks, foibles, follies, and even little triumphs
that so-called "ordinary" folks exhibit and experience every day.

Hardly headline stuff. It's the folks who rate maybe a three- or
four-inch squib piled in a stack of odd blurbs along the left margin and
buried somewhere inside the paper. These items report people and
events; for example, a woman suing McDonald's after a hot hamburger pickle burns her chin; a Tennessee guy single-handedly killing
his town's chance to have its own library; a high school senior struggling to raise big bucks for the privilege of conducting a major orches-

tra; a pair of brain-challenged felons sticking up places that had nothing to steal.

Inspiration for these subjects—and many others—come from news reports or, more often, from personal observation or a jaundiced eye that doesn't tolerate fools too easily. I'm intrigued by stories of ordinary people who stumble into extraordinary events. They get their fifteen minutes of glory (or chagrin, or discomfort, or rapture), then fade quickly into oblivion.

Politicians and heads of state, the ones who practice the "same old-same old" policies of bombast, blunder, and belligerence are, ultimately, boring. They're trapped by destiny, ambition, and ego. They have nowhere to go but down.

But when ordinary citizens are reported being heroic, magnanimous, creative, vengeful, or monumentally stupid, my literary saliva begins to flow. I want to capture and celebrate their achievements, however silly, noble, or puzzling. For just a moment in time, they stand out; they rise up. And there's no end to such achievements. There can't be—not so long as human beings act, well, human.

I could apologize for the mixed bag of subjects in this collection. But I won't. The only unifying theme is that these essays are all written by the same person, and the article "the" is often used to begin a lot of sentences.

How do you characterize a collection of essays that deals with a book-burning pastor, bumbling thieves, corporate crooks, fuzzy telephone bills, cranky computers, precocious pets, medical quackery, penny-pinching airlines, ingenious squirrels, hungry land developers, a laughable tax break for 80-year-olds, the origin of the paper clip, or the secret meanings of crossword puzzle clues. You can't. I know *I* can't.

It's society's fault. There are just too many unaccountable, unclassifiable, unexpected manifestations of human memory, action, and behavior in real life to be contained under a single label.

But that offers the reader a singular advantage. You don't have to read the book cover-to-cover. Dip in anywhere, roam, sample, taste. They're all short pieces, so you won't get stuck for too long.

My sincere thanks to the publications interested and gracious enough to first print the little essays that follow, notably *The Beaufort Gazette*, Beaufort, South Carolina, which published most of them over a four-year period; *Lowcountry Weekly* (still very much alive in Beaufort); *Beaufort Lowcountry Magazine* (no longer living, though I don't think I contributed to its demise); The *Charlotte* (NC) *Observer,* off and on for about six years; and *Center Arts*, a publication of the Civic Center Theatre Complex in Syracuse, NY, for about twenty years.

Animals In My Mailbox

Part One
Critters

Animals in my Mailbox

My wife is an animal lover of saintly proportions.

I guess I knew that when we married, but I indulged in the silly belief that *I* was the animal—a meat-eating rascal, an insatiably affectionate biped who loved to have his back scratched and tummy rubbed.

I was wrong. Her love was centered on the furry, four-footed variety—or two-footed if supplied with a pair of wings. I discovered my error when I asked her casually one day: "Honey, if both I and our Manx cat fell over the rail of a cruise ship, who would you toss a life jacket to?"

She paused. "Hmmm…"

Her affection for furry and feathered things is no act of phony virtue: she'd brave an ice storm to refill a bird feeder; she'd confront the growling backhoes of a construction crew to rescue and find homes for a litter of wild kittens; she'd challenge and threaten a corporate giant, decrying their use of live animals to test detergents. (No more Ivory Soap in *our* household!)

Several years ago, to put her money where her heart was, she sent a check to the SPCA. That's when it started; when first the trickle, then the deluge began; when our mailbox started to become swollen with heart-rending pleas to save the threatened, battered, abused, homeless, terrified, starving animals from the depredations of callous corporations, voracious developers, Oriental marketplaces, fighting pit bull promoters, poaching fishing trawlers, whale hunters, puppy mills, medical experimenters, and wolf killers.

Her name was somehow acquired by the Humane Society of the U.S. (Somehow? Or are mailing lists exchanged, purchased, or stolen?) My wife obligingly dispatched a small contribution to the HSUS. That pulled the cork out of the dike. ("We've got a live one, folks. She's a giver. Go get her!")

The Physicians Committee for Responsible Medicine (based in DC) let my wife know they're struggling to eliminate experiments on live animals, and for a modest $25.00 gift…

Finding homes for abandoned pets is the mission of the Northeast Animal Shelter (Salem, MA). Wouldn't my wife help to reverse the heartbreak of homeless cats?

Celebrities began to appear in our mailbox. First, the Doris Day Animal League (also in DC) urged my wife to take immediate action to impose sanitary regulations on puppy mills. A gift of $10.00 (or more) would do. And then Robert F. Kennedy slid into the mailbox as a spokesperson for the National Resources Defense Council (NYC), dedicated to protecting the majestic Gray Whale from the toxic waste that the Mitsubishi Corporation was threatening to spew into the whale nursery. They suggested a gift of $30.00.

And who could resist the heroics of the People for the Ethical Treatment Of Animals (Norfolk, VA) who have plucked dogs and cats from Hurricane Floyd's floodwaters, rescued monkeys from laboratories, and an aging elephant from a circus? (She could hardly ignore that one; after all, our son was, for a time, a PETA volunteer.)

Then she received an outraged plea from the World Society for the Protection of Animals (Jamaica Plain, MA) that featured photos of charred dogs under the headline, "Dogs burned alive in Asian meat markets!"

More dire and woeful solicitations arrived from the World Wildlife Fund (DC), the National Audubon Society (NYC), and the National Humane Education Society (Leesburg, VA), all three committed to preserve and protect wetlands, wildlife, forests, and wildlands; and from the Defenders of Wildlife (DC), who have adopted the sweeping commitment to protect *all* native wild animals and plants in their natural communities.

After receiving and digesting the pleas from all these (and other) agencies, we had several impressions surface: (a) there isn't an animal or bird—with the possible exception of, say, the Turkey Vulture— that isn't hurtling toward total extinction; (b) an animal is not a beast; man is; (c) to contribute to all the worthy supplicants in a meaningful way would devour our limited annual income and require periodic access to the U.S. Mint in DC, equipped with a shopping basket; and (d) have these agencies never heard of mergers, consolidations or United Appeal?

There is, however, a small reward for these occasional donations: calendars. Four-color, glossy-stock calendars featuring stunning photographs of adorable animals.

They are very nice. But what do you do with twelve calendars?

Pass the Friskies

The linear feet of supermarket shelves dedicated to Pet Products—dog, cat, bird, fish, gerbil—is not as long as a football field; it just seems that way. It's as long as Soups, longer than Bread, but shorter than Dry Cereals. I know. I've paced it off—one of the trivial and self-indulgent things a retired person is privileged to do while the wife over in Produce is gently pressing her thumbs on the polar ends of a cantaloupe.

We spend an inordinate amount of time at the cat food section, hoping to predict which variety of irresistible flavor combinations might excite the palate of our imperious, aging and cranky Manx pussycat. Like we are, she's a senior citizen that requires—so our Vet declares—a healthful, balanced and digestible diet. The label on the cat food can, we are solemnly instructed, must say "Senior."

The manufacturers of Friskies, Whiskas, 9 Lives, and Sheba are pretty wily critters themselves. The product labels are really designed to whet the palate of people, not cats. A cat wouldn't know a tuna if it got whacked on the head by one. A cat wouldn't know a Chicken and Mackerel Feast, a Savory Duck in Meaty Juice, or Sardines, Shrimp and Crab in Jelly from a hairball.

But we bipeds do. Ah, that Savory Duck—yum-yum. Oh, that Turkey and Cheese in Gravy—slurp-slurp. Maybe if we just sprinkle a little garlic powder on that canned grayish glob, maybe drop an anchovy or two on top, it might make a tasty and cheap hors d'oeuvre at a dinner party. Guests might end the meal by wiping their lips, in the manner of fastidious cats, with the moistened side of their thumbs.

At one time, we had three pet cats—Fergie, Andy and Charlie (all named in deference to the British Royal Family)—which made the business of selecting a food variety acceptable to all three a maddening and masochistic process. Those fickle beasts taunted us. On Monday, all three greedily devoured the Tuna Supreme. On Tuesday, all three sniffed at it suspiciously—as if we had laced the food with cyanide. They'd turn their backs on it and begin scratching the floor as if trying to bury it. Failing to obliterate the tuna, they began a series of mournful and cacophonous yowls that seemed to ask the pseudo-Biblical question: Why have you forsaken us?

We finally hit upon a solution that satisfied and delighted them. Instead of going to the cat food section of the market, we went to the deli. There we purchased a pound of Boars Head turkey pastrami. The cats were ecstatic. Like in Cat Heaven. They stood and danced on their hind legs. Crankiness and yowling vanished. We could have sworn we heard them laughing.

Our Vet, however, was not amused.

Back to the Tuna Supreme.

Save the Worms

If I knew I would trigger a landslide, I'd have never sent the fifteen bucks.

That's all it took. Actually, it was my wife who prodded me a few years ago to send the modest gift to the Humane Society of the U.S. (Her priorities are eminently clear: if a man and a dog were both about to drown, she'd toss a rope to the dog—persuading me never to jump overboard with a Cocker Spaniel.)

The $15.00 gift instantly identified me—along the pulsating, inter-connected computer pathways shared by a multitude of do-good agen-cies—as a Live One, a Mark, an Animal Hugger, a Planet Protector.

Après the small donation, *le deluge!*

Maudlin appeals began to mount in my mailbox, each with a cata-log of baleful tales about the dwindling elephant population, homeless lion cubs, hunted wolves, threatened whales, bulldozed wetlands, vanishing coral reefs. The specter of global extinction lurked behind every heart-wrenching calamity.

With at least fifteen national organizations dedicated to reversing those calamities, you'd think that no crawling, swimming, flying, or flowering thing has been overlooked.

Not so. There are three of God's creatures that need urgent and im-mediate help.

I've begun drafting by-laws for the creation of the Annelid Conser-vancy League of America. After all, no flora or fauna could survive without the efforts of a blind, squiggly, noble, soil-aerating earth-worm. My neighbor understands; I spotted him smiling broadly as he dug in his garden. "I've got worms!" he declared proudly.

And how empty would be the childhood of ruddy little boys denied the thrill of skewering a worm on a fish hook, or evoking a "Yech!" from a little girl as he dangles one in her face.

The motto of the Annelid League: The Lowest Shall be the Highest. If the snail darter can halt construction of a multi-million dollar dam, surely an earthworm should be protected from the deadly trenching machine of cable TV installers.

Once the paperwork is filed, my next goal is the formation of the TVADF—the Turkey Vulture Anti-Defamation Fund. An ugly bird?

Bite your tongue. Rapacious, maybe; some vulgar habits, perhaps; and not exactly a Robert Redford face. But vigilant, resourceful and determined to fulfill its manifest destiny as one of Nature's preeminent Cleaner-Uppers.

Without the unique dietary habits of the Turkey Vulture, roadkill would rival beer cans as a national hazard and disgrace. If the Turkey Vulture has a motto, it would surely be: "It's a dirty job, but something has to do it."

The new Anti-Defamation Fund would focus on softening the creature's image: scenes of vulture family life; nest-building; delivering tasty snacks to their young; outings to the shore; comforting an ailing friend. A few cosmetic improvements—a nose job, maybe—and the Turkey Vulture might one day aspire to the heroic and popular image of the American Eagle.

With the Earthworm and the Turkey Vulture now securely ensconced as cherished species, worthy of respect and generous contributions, the final step is the formation of the SPCSG—the Society for the Prevention of Cruelty to Sand Gnats, a truly prolific, persistent and pervasive creation of a cranky Mother Nature. Though tiny, the burden they bear is gargantuan, as any resident of the Lowcountry will testify. They breed with Biblical magnitude, as if sneering at the contempt they rouse in harassed humans. They are intelligent, appearing only in the most salubrious climate, sharing with humans the delight in fair weather. They are therapeutic, causing the heart muscle to strengthen, the blood circulation to improve by virtue of the rapid flailing of arms and flapping of hands to dispel them.

And Sand Gnats are artistic: the prickly kisses they imprint on exposed arms and legs often form delightful patterns of red spots that would rival the skill of an abstract painter.

My three new critter defense associations will begin soliciting funds within the next six months. The appeals—touching and irresistible—will be accompanied by enticing gifts: a car window decal (depicting the mating dance of the gnat), a calendar (twelve months in the life of a Turkey Vulture), and note cards (embossed with worm tracks).

I'm reasonably certain all gifts will be declared tax-deductible.

Ghost Cat, Dead Fish

It was totally unforeseen. Our retirement plan was gloriously simple: do nothing. Unwind, sleep late, snicker at working stiffs, watch a drawbridge open, see our grass mowed (by someone else), and indulge in the sacrament of cocktails at five o'clock.

In short, disengage. That was the plan.

In subtle and curious ways, the plan changed, showing us how vulnerable retirees are to the polite overtures of neighbors who need small services performed while they're away for a few hours, overnight, a couple of days, two weeks. Retirees are, after all, well, retired. They're mostly at home, so it hardly seems like a rude imposition to request a little neighborly assistance. Indeed, the request could be viewed as a morale-booster to Seniors who will feel productive by house-watching; child-tending; fish-, cat-, dog-, gerbil-feeding; plant-watering; mail- and newspaper-collecting. A new, unanticipated career, not described in any Manual on Feeling Useful after 65.

Of all the surrogate tasks we're asked to perform, however, surely it's the pet-feeding that offers the most rewarding, often puzzling, and sometimes depressing experience. Two examples:

Kashmere (sic) the Ghost Cat.

She's a neighbor's Siamese, a cat bred for centuries to be sly, imperial, elusive. At least we *think* there's a cat named Kashmere living next door. Wife Lucy, who acts as the mother figure, dishes up the morning and evening servings of dry and wet food when the owner is absent. Lucy swears she has actually seen the pussycat, fleetingly: a nose, an ear tip, a tail flip.

Timid and reclusive, the cat evidently views strangers with caution, if not outright hostility. Oh, we've searched—under the bed, behind the sofa, on top of cabinets. But Kashmere possesses, we suspect, the ability to dematerialize. Or she's constructed in the depths of a linen closet her own Transporter Room, and beams up to the Crab Nebula whenever an alien voice, step, or smell enters the house. Ghost or not, she certainly loves her Deli-Cat. We've accused our neighbor of perpetrating a fiction. The cat is a hologram. It's the neighbor who devours Deli-Cat.

Another client: Goldfish—A Death in the Family.

We agreed to feed the fish for two weeks while their masters, we jealously reflected, vacationed up in Cape Cod. Three fish to be serviced: Ike, Mike and Billy. On our first feeding visit, Ike and Mike were gaily darting and swooping in the tank, happily anticipating the imminent meal. Billy, however, was eerily immobile, its nose pointing downward at a 45-degree angle. We tapped gently on the glass; no movement. We sprinkled in the food. Ike and Mike dashed for it; Billy hung motionlessly. With a small net, we nudged Billy. Nothing. We'd been warned that Billy was "sickly." Billy had moved beyond sickly. Billy was dead.

The fish had clearly shuffled off its piscine coil and passed over to where Neptune dwelt in a watery heaven. But what to do with the remains? Recalling a Cosby Show TV episode, Lucy and I assembled around the commode and solemnly dropped Billy into the bowl. I can't recall if sacred words were spoken or last rites performed before I pressed the handle and flushed him away. (What if Billy really wasn't dead, we pondered later. Would Billy revive in the sewer system and, like baby alligators, feed and feed and grow into an 80-foot monster, someday bursting the lid of a storm sewer and terrorizing the good people of Beaufort? How will the City Council cope with a rampant, marauding 200-pound goldfish? By producing an Ordinance, of course, banning 200-pound goldfish within the City limits.)

Flushing away a fish was not our retirement plan. But, we like our neighbors and their kids. We love animals. We cherish growing green things. And we're especially intrigued by what catalogs our neighbors get in the mail.

Besides, we now enjoy a lengthy roster of folks who *owe us* when we take off for a day, a week, a month… *Quid Pro Quo* is a delightful concept.

Yummy Moles

As a city boy, the only mole I ever saw was the little dark lump on the left side of my Aunt Rose's nose. The notion that a mole was some furry, deaf, mostly blind critter that burrowed underground tunnels in a garden was alien to me. Being an urban kid, who knew from a garden?

But I have one now. And the telltale signs are beginning to appear. Soft squishy mounds are rising under the layer of pine straw. Step on one and it feels like the earth is sinking under your foot. You can almost trace the path of the mole as it applies its shovel-like forefeet to open underground passageways in its unquenchable quest for food.

There are, my trusty Internet sources tell me, some 30 species of mole worldwide, with seven of the 30 making their home in North America. Judging by the number of visible holes, serpentine tunnel shapes and squishy mounds, all seven North American varieties have taken up residence in my garden, and have issued invitations to the other twenty-three.

Well, as long as these members of Family *Talpidae* confine their menu to munching earthworms and assorted dirt-dwelling insects, my resident moles and I will try to coexist in a state of wary entente.

But let the moles start nibbling—as some mole species do—on the delicate, defenseless and vulnerable roots of my darling, newly-planted (and expensive) artemesia, agapanthus, mahonia or abelia sherwoodi—and the ominous drumbeat of war will thunder through the soil. The unprintable expletives I will hurl at them will, unfortunately, fall on deaf ears.

Veterans of the Mole Wars offer combat suggestions: Moletox, a substance the label guarantees will force the moles to seek asylum in Iraq; rat poison—a few crystals down the mole hole; and Sonic Vibrators, a product from England where, one supposes, the prolonged exposure to high frequency tones is the root cause of stiff upper lips.

If moles are global, abundant, mischievous, and sometimes destructive, it's foolhardy to engage in warfare.

Better idea: eat them.

Maybe the U.S. Department of Agriculture will award a huge grant to USC to study and determine the nutritional value of moles. Could they be a new source of unsaturated fat, of protein or carbohydrates? And if so, perhaps they will begin to appear on the menus of *haute cuisine* restaurants as Puree of Mole with Arugula, Mole Puttanesca alla Venezia (a nice Pinot Grigio is suggested), Mole Encrusted Broiled Tilapia, Pate of Mole or Mole Vinaigrette with Chick Peas and Truffles.

Instead of Big Mac, Big Mole.

Why not? People eat squirrel, alligator, possum and chocolate-covered ants.

And moles should be easy to capture: they can't hear, so you don't have to sneak up on them; they can barely see, or not see at all, so no camouflage needed.

With millions of people on the planet going hungry—and millions of gardeners going crazy—this may be a workable solution.

We must not waste the resources that Nature has so generously provided.

Let 'Em Eat Birdseed

Wily. Rapacious. Destructive.

Squirrels.

There has to be something redeeming about them, but it's hard to find. They are hairy, insolent, ubiquitous rodents that twitch a bushy tail at me in arrogant contempt of my role as property owner, taxpayer, and U.S. Citizen.

I never objected to having them share the planet with me—or me with them. But that didn't extend to sharing my innocent tomatoes.

I have no killer instinct. I don't own a weapon of any kind. But seeing my scrupulously nurtured garden littered with tomato corpses made me dream of an AK47.

For a lot of summers, just as my tomatoes were subtly changing from green to red, and we started fantasizing about fresh sliced tomato and onion sandwiches with mayo—the beasts attacked, randomly gnawing and munching on the helpless fruit.

I can be sympathetic to starving four-legged creatures. But these critters didn't *eat* the tomatoes. They'd just bite a chunk, suck the liquid from the fruit, and casually toss the remains aside.

Having declared my dislike, distrust, and dismay toward *genus sciurus*, I'll confess in fairness that the critter has one redeeming feature: an unrelenting persistence. They are driven to overcome any obstacle that blocks their pathway to free snacks.

We recently installed a bird feeder just outside our breakfast area window. (Can you predict the end of this tale?) It hangs on a metal post, which stands 80" high, shaped like a shepherd's crook. An arm at the top of the post extends 12" from which the feeder is hung, 15" below the arm. Squirrel-proof, right?

It wasn't long before Frick, one of a pair of resident backyard squirrels (the other named Frack, of course, in a modest salute to a team of vaudeville greats) discovered the challenge and set to work.

It was tough. At first, Frick struggled, its clawed feet grabbing the slippery metal pole, fighting to claim a foothold. It quit several times, squeezing its primitive brain for clever strategies. But Frick, we realized, possessed an indomitable spirit and an empty stomach.

We didn't see Frick's moment of triumph. But when we looked out a few minutes later, there he was, his hairy body draped over the top of the feeder, his mouth buried in the seed tray, and his tail, like a defiant banner, quivering in squirrelly glory.

We hope the local avian population is tolerant of this assault on its supplemental food source.

Anyway, better the birdseed than my tomatoes.

The Protector

If my wife had her own Coat of Arms, it would depict a dog, cat and deer rampant on a field in Eden. And in bold letters her personal motto would declare: Love Animals–Hate People. It would be written in English, not Latin, so you wouldn't miss the point.

Translation of motto: man has become the most predatory, unfeeling, cruel and destructive enemy of nature's most exquisite creatures. It's people who have decimated entire species of animals, have driven them from their natural habitats (1,200 new houses and a golf course on the way) and have subjected them to experiments for beauty and household products that would receive the enthusiastic approval of Dr. Mengele.

If she had been the first female resident in the Garden of Eden, she and the Serpent would have become pals, holding afternoon chats about angels, loincloths, and applesauce.

If she'd lived in Biblical times, she'd have lobbied Moses to add an 11th Commandment: Thou Shalt Love, Cherish and Protect the Beasts of the Field and the Birds of the Air.

No empty philosophy here; no cocktail party small talk.

She's defied earthmovers and backhoes to rescue litters of endangered wild kittens; braved chill winds and icy rains to keep bird feeders filled; dispatched righteous letters to mega-corporations to protest their practice of squirting liquid soap into the eyes of dogs and cats.

She's no nut. Her credo is awesomely simple: the God that created humans created animals. To kill, abuse or dispossess man or beast is an abiding cardinal sin. Quite a sane piece of reasoning, actually, though not widely accepted.

I totally support her passion to protect and nurture animals of all kinds. My support of wildlife, on the other hand, is focused on crawly and stingy things—spiders, ants, wasps, *et al*. In fact, I've struck a deal with these species, a kind of détente (as they say in diplomatic circles). The arrangement is: when you critters are happily occupying and operating on your turf—outdoors—I'll respect and protect you. But if you should invade my turf—kitchen, bathroom, closet—out comes the Raid. Unless, of course, you're prepared to pick up a little of the monthly mortgage payment.

If I should kick my bucket before my wife kicks hers, I would hope for instant reincarnation. I'd want to return as her ideal pet—a gentle, loveable but fiercely protective German Shepherd/Beagle hybrid. She won't know it happened until, mystically, she's drawn to the local SPCA where I'll be waiting. I know she'll come. I'd still be slightly damp from the amniotic fluid in which reincarnated husbands float for awhile.

She'll know it's me. Especially if my tail wags fervently when presented with a dish of liver and onions, or a salami-and-egg sandwich on a bagel. Or, as a special treat, a tasty morsel of a sweet, chocolaty Devil Dog. Oh, she'll know.

I don't think she'll let me sleep with her in the same bed—you know, dirty paws, fleas maybe, and the occasional olfactory emanation that dogs produce sometimes.

That's OK. I'll settle for a place on the floor next to the bed.

I'll be safe.

Protect the Tiger

Homeland security has to begin with security of one's home. No, this isn't a plug for ADT, Brinks, or any other enterprise that will arm your house with bells, sirens and whistles that shriek collectively if a predator so much as burps at your back door.

One's house is, as they say, one's castle, sanctuary and bulwark against sneaky villains who threaten property and peace of mind.

For Ray Cox, over in Greenville County, installing complex wiring, secret codes or keypads to protect his trailer home was never an option. He didn't need a complicated high-tech system from ADT or Brinks.

All he needed for total security was his companion Gwen.

Gwen is his pet, purchased in 1999 when she was very tiny. She now weighs 500 pounds.

Gwen is Roy's Bengal Tiger—a jungle creature often described as cunning, ruthless, and majestic.

Understandably, his neighbors are unimpressed with her majestic traits. They're nervous—especially those whose kids have to pass Gwen's cage on their way to school every morning.

Greenville County officials, reacting to agitated neighbors, have demanded that Gwen's owner show proof of $50,000 in liability insurance—an amount, evidently, that underwriters have assessed as the monetary value of a neighbor kid who Gwen might enjoy as a mid-day snack.

In addition to his carnivorous pussycat, Mr. Cox' back-up security was a collection of snakes—species and dietary customs unspecified. Had County officials known about his ophidian interests, they might have upped the insurance premium. But not a problem. The snakes were recently swapped for an assortment of guns.

Mr. Cox is obviously no dummy. Gwen represents a substantial investment that, like any family asset, needs protecting. That double electrified fence enclosing Gwen's 20 x 40-foot cage was a pricey item. Gwen, like most Bengal or White tigers, will gobble up 40 pounds of meat in one meal, causing Mr. Cox to pore over weekly beef specials at Publix or Piggly Wiggly.

38

There's the monthly visit by a vet who checks Gwen's heart, lungs, teeth and bowel movements. And the periodic visits by a certified tiger shrink whose task is to persuade Gwen to abandon her jungle instincts and rediscover her sweet inner child.

The guns are simply to protect Gwen against hunters who, after a quart of Bombay Gin, mistake Greenville County for the virgin forests of Bangladesh or Nepal. And the neighbor kids, growing up with the friendly, frisky image of Tony the Tiger on a cereal box, might tease and provoke Gwen into ignoring her sweet inner child.

So it's not the Cox mobile home that needs the services of ADT or Brinks. It's Gwen.

But for ultimate security, and as an act of enlightened compassion, Mr. Cox might consider sending Gwen back to her jungle pals in Bangladesh, India, Nepal or Bhutan. Or at least to a civilized zoo.

Where she belongs.

Animals in my Mailbox II

I thought I had slain the dragon. Wrong.

I failed to realize that scaly, ill-tempered and insatiable dragons, being mythological creatures, never die.

Back in '99, I wrote what I thought was a feisty, incisive, snarky piece on the avalanche of heart-breaking appeals that almost daily filled my mailbox. They were often gut-wrenching solicitations, begging money to save, rescue and protect creatures with wings, fins or four legs. Definitely non-mythical critters.

In dramatic words and pictures, they pleaded for help to save the threatened, battered, abused, homeless, terrified or starving land, air and sea creatures. They depicted the depredations of callous corporations, voracious developers, Oriental market places, pit bull fighting promoters, vanishing coral reefs, poaching fishing trawlers, whale hunters, puppy mills, medical experimenters, wolf killers, and stallion starvers.

As a threatened species myself (toxic wastes, terrorist attacks, carcinogens in French fries, and the marauding highway hazard of SUVs) it was easy to identify with threatened sea otters or adorable hippos.

In the '99 piece, I offered a modest proposal. Because my capacity to support the squadrons of worthy causes is, at best, limited, and because I'm disinclined to steal Social Security checks, rob banks, or stick up school kids for their lunch money in order to rescue sick turkeys (see below), I offered a modest and realistic solution to the growing plague of requests.

Emulate corporate titans: merge, consolidate, and amalgamate. Create a single national United Way to foster wildlife creatures and habitats.

Being one of America's most lucrative growth industries, wildlife defenders have greeted the proposal with passionate indifference. Like a lead balloon, actually. Well, maybe they don't subscribe to *The Beaufort Gazette*.

They not only ignored my cogent suggestion—as I knew they would—but a cluster of new puppy-panda-parrot protectors have appeared on the scene, their hands (or paws) out for the generous contribution they're confident I'll dispatch at once.

In Bakersfield, CA, The Lifesavers Wild Horse Rescue Ranch hoped I'd be equally outraged over the cruel and inhumane treatment of wild mustangs. A $50.00 donation would be just right.

The Best Friends Animal Sanctuary in Kenab, Utah, views any support of wildlife best friends as a "miracle of love."

One of the newer kids on the block, Oceana, out of D.C., has adopted a planetary goal: restore and protect the world's oceans and all of their inhabitants. A gift of $25.00 or more....

My favorite new creature comforter is the Rescue and Refuge Fund in Watkins Glen, NY—an organization that claims it freed 100 sick and crippled turkeys from a salvage yard promoter. With my generous contribution, they will cure and rehabilitate the gobblers in anticipation, perhaps, of a profitable Thanksgiving holiday.

Long-range financial planning is the latest wrinkle among several wildlife protectors. How about, they seductively suggest, authorizing automatic monthly transfers of funds from your checking account? Why not put our bighorn sheep and buffalo in your will? Or can we persuade you to set up a trust fund to ensure a happy and productive future for polar bears, foxes, and mountain lions?

The goal of these agencies is worthy and honorable. But why, oh why, don't they join together into one overpowering and irresistible pitch?

Well, no more free advice to the two dozen wildlife wonks. They had their chance.

Besides, our Manx cat has made it abundantly clear: forget sea otters. Charity begins at home.

Part Two
Human Critters

Inflammatory Pickle

Now tell the truth—what would *you* do?

There you are, slowly raising a McDonald's Quarter Pounder to your mouth, inhaling the exotic essence of seared steer flesh, succulent onions, melted cheese, and crisply toasted bun. You're ready for that first bite and anticipating the gustatory delight of devouring a veritable American fast-food icon, when suddenly—

Terror! Pain! Outrage!

An errant and malicious slice of pickle squirts out of the bun and lands on your chin. Not just an ordinary, docile pickle, mind you, but a *hot* pickle. Blazing hot, a Knoxville woman complained recently—hotter evidently than the fiery regions of Dante's Inferno.

You scream in pain, or perhaps in surprise, but your attorney will insist that you suffered unbearable, remorseless, scarring, withering pain.

Your chin now bears a pickle imprint. Your attractive features have become, like Dorian Gray's, decayed and disfigured. How will you ever face your family or friends with your pickle-seared chin? Will your spouse ever find you attractive again, or turn away in revulsion? What will you do?

Hire an attorney and sue McDonald's, of course. And why not? After all, a few years ago a customer won a juicy settlement from McDonald's when a cup of hot coffee cascaded onto the customer's crotch. (Later known in legal parlance as the Cooked Crotch Litigation.) Why shouldn't a hot pickle, the law suit read, from a "defective and unreasonably dangerous" hamburger produce a healthy pile of bucks for the Knoxville woman? A $110,000 pile.

Her husband, who evidently thought his wife's chin was her primary erogenous zone, was seeking $15,000 for being deprived of his wife's "services and consortium." (Remarkable. In the 5,000-year annals of sexual relations there has never been a report of a man being titillated by a woman's chin. Feet, fingers, neck...but never chin.)

Yet there are lawsuits more bizarre than the Pickle Plaintiff.

Several years ago a lady sued a carmaker because the vehicle's engine had the audacity to conk out as she was trying to depart this vale of tears with carbon monoxide. Frustrated and angry by the failed attempt, she sued the manufacturer for thwarting her suicidal impulse. And won.

Or the man with the apparent mentality of a retarded baboon who picked up his power mower while the blade was still spinning, instantly shortening several fingers. He sued. And won.

It seems that the only thing more limitless than outer space is man's aptitude for exploitation, stupidity, skullduggery, and irrational anger. A neighbor's branch falls in your yard shattering a ceramic flower pot. Sue 'em. A fly is discovered doing the backstroke in your martini. Sue the pub. Your plump kid is bumped off the school's track team. Sue the School Board. Courts are jammed. Settlements can take years. But the passionate love affair with litigation gets hotter and hotter.

Ah, for the bad old days of swift remedies for bad actions. A face slapped with kid gloves meant rapiers at sunrise. A face-off at high noon between Sheriff Goodheart and Black Bart settled a bank heist. A contract hit on a crooked crook, fitted with cement shoes, silenced a squealer.

It might have been refreshing if the bruised Knoxville lady had challenged the manager to a duel—hot apple pie at 30 paces.

Computer Blues

The message had a kind of catastrophic finality about it. It read: "A fatal exception OE has occurred at O18F: BFF9DFFF."

I raced to the bookshelf for my copy of *Windows For Dummies*. I looked up "fatal;" nothing. "Exception;" nothing. I searched for "OE" and "O18f." I scoured the pages looking for any reference that contained the letter "F" at least five times. A blank.

It was a dire warning, obviously crafted by a bearded, bespectacled, t-shirted, hostile nerd wearing a bathing cap and sitting in a dank sub-basement of the Microsoft complex. In an eerie corner of this chamber was, I imagined, a Rack, an Iron Maiden, and several other machines of torture too horrible to describe.

Despite the risk, I deleted the fatal message, and found I was in water hotter than before. Up on the screen flashed: "SOL caused a general protection fault in module USER.EXE at 0007: 000083f9. Registers: EAX=00ffffff CS: 1797 EIP 000083f9EFLGS: 00000 205." OK, so who the devil is this SOL? And why is this SOL messing around with my 00ffffff?

Urdu, Hindi, Sumerian, Celtic, Serbo-Croatian—human cultures on planet earth have spawned dozens, even hundreds of languages that have seemed weird, exotic, enigmatic, musical. Some survived, many vanished.

But none so exasperatingly obscure, constipated, unpoetic, and so utterly, indecipherably remote from human experience as the language manufactured by the boys and girls sitting in little cubicles and communicating in icons, digits, ports, protocols, faults, and modules.

Look closely at these boys and girls. See the tiny star-shaped mole tucked under their left earlobes? They are aliens, delivered as spores to a vacant Edsel assembly plant in northern Minnesota where they're bred as computer language intimidators.

They've accomplished a lot in twenty-five years—concocting not one, but over twenty incomprehensible languages: COBOL, Dylan, Eclipse, Eiffel, Fortran, Occam, Prolog, REXX, Sisal, and more.

Clearly the languages they contrive are written for each other.

Why else would my computer screen warn me: "Protocol POP3, Port 110. Secure (SSL): No, Socket Error: 11001, Error Number Ox 800ccc00."

And why, out of the blue, would my sinister machine threaten me with the question: "Do you want to install and run IPX 35676. EXE?" To run *what?*

I have a dream. Someday a civilized computer will come on the market, one that rediscovers the English language. And when I mess up, the screen will gently and humanely say: "Joey, baby...you hit the wrong key again. Stay calm, and watch that pinky finger on your right hand. Got it?" I nod.

"Attaboy!"

Garagescapes

The garage has surely become one of the greater architectural abominations of the twentieth century—especially when it's plunked down at the front of a house, virtually obliterating the human habitation. And as the garage has swollen from the one-car, to the two-car, and then the three-car, with its bland, characterless doors facing the street, housing for our sacred four-wheel objects has slowly, insidiously, begun to dominate the property. It has, indeed, turned many neighborhoods from streetscapes into garagescapes.

In a syndicated article that appeared in *The Gazette* last September, Laura Christman reminded us that the bulky object we call a garage has a venerable ancestry: the barn (to shelter cows and horses) which evolved into the shed (to park the buggy). It then got attached to the house as a repository for autos and the dozen other appurtenances of the good life—boats, sports equipment, hobby workshop, kids' bikes. The garage door had become the front door.

And as the garage expanded, it got harder to squeeze it onto a standard lot—without thrusting it out front. It was inevitable that a 24-foot-wide garage would be the dominant feature of a 50 to 60-foot-wide house.

When a garage overwhelms a residence, the structural and aesthetic distinction of the house has been compromised.

It won't be long before an ad will appear in *The Gazette* that reads:

> Spectacular Opportunity! Tasteful and sturdy four-car garage on marshfront property. Low-country styling, three dormers, and Palladian windows with Country Curtain treatment. Fully landscaped. Several live oaks, dripping with Spanish Moss adjacent to garage complex. Loft space, suitable for mother-in-law or grandparent apartment, supplied with decorator gas masks to protect occupants against carbon monoxide.
>
> Birch paneling throughout. State-of-the-art heat pump to ensure safe vehicle environment. Anti-theft alarm system. Basketball hoops installed over each of the four doors for father-son quality time. Convenient to hospital, shopping and bowling alley. Interior amenities: storage area, workshop, exercise corner (rowing

machine included), sauna, half bath, and wet bar. Motion-sensing lights activate as cars approach doors. Community-Association approved. Dock permit in hand. Bonus space: three-bedroom, two-bath living quarters suitable for human habitation, only one-quarter of which is visible from the street in order not to startle or offend the sensibilities of neighbors. Priced for quick sale at $375,500. Contact: Mike Piston, BIC, Overhead Door Realty.

Stamp 'Em Out!

There is a sinister conspiracy afoot, and I—as a mature and responsible adult—feel obliged to expose it.

I'm not a whistle-blower by nature, but this threat must be brought to the attention of the American public before Western Civilization is forever compromised.

Quietly and insidiously, the world is being taken over by kids.

These boys and girls, who seem to be just barely through puberty, or maybe just entering it, are occupying positions of authority and influence to a degree that is alarming. Have you noticed it? And with every year that passes, they get younger and younger.

I began to detect this global conspiracy about ten years ago when I was hospitalized briefly for some tests. The doctor was expected momentarily—which means anywhere from fifteen minutes to the next millennium. A figure eventually approached and said, "Hi, I'm Doctor_____." I was expecting a kindly, gentle, wise, slightly plump, gray-haired Gene Hersholt or Marcus Welby type. What a shock. I looked up to see a skinny, wire-haired kid who probably shaved for the first time in his life that very morning. A *kid*! He could have been a grandson just back from a Cub Scout hike in the woods. A *baby*! I wanted to get off the examining table and look for the teddy bear he'd probably sewed up inside the abdominal cavity of his last patient.

From that moment on, and with every passing year, the Kid Cult has been gaining strength.

About five years ago, I wandered into a concert hall to hear a little of a symphony orchestra rehearsal. There, on the podium, arms flailing, leading a very sophisticated ensemble in a deeply complex piece (Mahler, I think), was a twelve-year-old boy. Well, he *looked* twelve. I swear he'd probably never dated or kissed a girl. He couldn't have been old enough to pitch for the Little League. Did he have his mother's permission to wave that stick at the musicians?

A year ago, while shopping, I asked to see the manager of a very large supermarket. An adolescent boy approached. I could almost believe I spotted traces of Beechnut Mashed Apricots on his chin and a little acne on his forehead. The kid is controlling a two-million-dollar inventory and 150 employees?

And I get especially unnerved when I see an airline pilot who looks younger than my son. The pilot ought to be building model planes rather than flying monster metal ones.

We're being surrounded, engulfed, overwhelmed by kids. Where have all the grownups gone? I know this is a youth-oriented society (look at who guzzles all those soft drinks or gorges on potato chips in TV commercials), but is there no limit to the onslaught of baby-faced, energetic, talented, flat-tummied, slim-hipped, burbling babes? I'm tempted to write to my Congressional delegation and urge them to establish a new federal agency: The Office of Youth Suppression.

If I have to entrust my body, mind, and stomach to a stranger, is it too much to ask that the stranger be at least 55? Or *look* 55?

There's an easy way, however, to deal with my feelings of intimidation and paranoia. All I have to do is candidly confront the issue and say, "They're not getting young. I'm getting...."

No. Never. Rather than admit the truth, I'll stick to the idea of a sinister conspiracy, in the magnitude of, say, the Inquisition.

I've got one thing going for me, though, and it offers me some comfort. I haven't dribbled Mashed Apricots on my chin for...well...for over a week.

Blessings From Columbia

They've given me something to look forward to. To live for.

Our State Legislature—commonly known as those squirrelly whipper-snappers in Columbia—have shown an unimaginable degree of compassionate generosity to older South Carolinians.

If you're 85 or older, that is.

The little sign in many stores proclaims: "Individuals 85 years old. You are entitled to a 1% state sales tax reduction on items purchased for your personal use. You must ask for the reduction and present proof of your age at the cash register."

The Honorables at the Capitol clearly don't want any sneaky, avaricious 84-year-old ripping off the state taxation department by trying to pass for 85.

My secret informant in Columbia shared with me certain provisions of the one-percent break for seniors that were deleted on the second and third readings of the Bill:

If confined to a wheelchair, 1.1% off; if attached to a portable respirator, 1.2% off; if accompanied by a health care provider of Haitian ancestry, 1.3% off.

The State Merchants Association lobbied against and killed the add-on provisions. Shop clerks, they argued, would take too long to calculate 1.3% of $28.72, especially given the level of mathematical competence of the State's public school graduates.

It's true, of course, that 85-year-olds ain't what they used to be. Medical advances, improved diets, and exercise programs more challenging than checkers have increased the inventory of able-bodied 85ers. There will still be, alas, some less alert who, if they can get to a store at all, won't see or can't read the small print on the sign; who will be puzzled over what's "personal use" (a gift for a grandchild is not personal?); who may or may not remember to carry proof of age (how often does an 85-year-old get carded at a bar?); or where such proof is tucked away in a wallet or purse; or who may have no taste or patience for idle blather about their age with an indifferent cash register clerk.

But the Legislature's relentless pursuit of political decisions that cultivate the goodwill of senior citizens will not be diminished by such trivial concerns.

It's rumored that at the next session of the Legislature, the discount net will be widened: a 90-year-old S.C. citizen will be allowed a two percent sales tax reduction on any surfboard purchased on a Thursday between 6:30 and 7:00 A.M. Ninety-five-year-olds who can prove they are ambulatory may expect a three-percent tax break on the purchase of any bungee rope—for personal use only.

And at 100, expect total exemption from sales tax on the entry fee, decorated jump suit, pit crew and ambulance service at the 2003 Indy 500—if purchased in Aiken.

The sensitivity and generosity of State Legislators to the Grey Panther population knows no limits.

I can barely wait for the tax break on my bungee cord.

Into the Woods

Wilderness training is strongly recommended to anyone planning to build a house. It will prepare you for surviving a strange and confusing environment for six to eight months, equipped only with aspirin, checkbook, and an October, 1987 copy of *House Beautiful*. It'll make you painfully conscious of how ill-prepared you are to enter the mysterious terrain, the tortuous landscape of home construction; how grossly lacking in survival skills for encountering the three specters that lurk—like the Blair Witch—in the planning forest: the Designer, the Builder, and the Code Enforcer.

How you wish you'd won a Scout Merit Badge for building a birdhouse, or at least changing a light bulb!

The first specter, the Designer, stabs at a key that revs up his CAD (Computer-Assisted Design) software. We quickly discover that he's from another solar system. He communicates, imperially, in a language that would make a PhD in Linguistics tremble. "The cove molding around the vaulted ceiling will be above the soffits. The moisture barrier is applied right after the piers are sunk. We'll adjust the footprint for the plat. The double-hung windows need mullions. The tempered glass must have a U-Factor of 4, and will need lateral transoms. The siding can be ChemPlank or HardiBoard. Rheostats for fans with a sone rating not to exceed 2.5. Decide: gliders, terrace, or French doors. Rain diverters or drip chains? In wet areas, ground fault interrupters, of course. Ready to begin?"

Numbed by a vocabulary as esoteric as Sanskrit, and now armed with a thirteen-page roll of plans tucked under our moist armpits, we stumble over to…The Builder, a gregarious fellow who assures us that our site is a delight, the soil is sound, the design is dandy and doable, and we can easily survive the setback. The what? "Oh, yes…you gotta be 50 feet back from the water, 25 feet in from the road, and 10 feet in from each side." From a post card size, the lot just shrank to a postage stamp.

His crew? "Hey, top of the line, A-number-one! My electrician's been with me since Edison invented the light bulb (chuckle). My plumber hasn't had a leak in twenty years (bigger chuckle). And don't you believe stories about the Japanese buying up all the plywood and drywall. I got a supplier (wink, wink) in Boise…. And don't worry about Permits. I have a Permanent Permit that allows me to Request Permits (loud chuckle)."

"And boy are you lucky! Not a Live Oak on the property! We can just drive in and whack out any tree we want. Look like the Salt Flats in eight minutes!" We groan helplessly at the impending brutal attack.

How long will it take to build? "Well, depending on the weather, available manpower, delivery of materials, and Alan Greenspan, anywhere from six to eight months. "Course, I got three construction jobs underway right now…Hurricane Mordecai out there…But can definitely start your dream house by June, 2002."

In August, 2002, the Code Enforcers begin to infiltrate the building site. Armed with compass, slide rule, magnifying glass, sextant, transit, and Ouija Board, they discover that the 50-foot setback from the creek's critical line measures only 49 feet, 11-15/16 inches. Aha! A violation. A report, in quadruplicate, will reach you at about the time the asphalt shingles are being nailed to the roof, insisting that the house be moved 1/16th of an inch; that you cease and desist from further construction; and that you don't even *think* about dumping 50 truckloads of fill at the water's edge to recover the missing 16th of an inch.

Oh, and by the way, the amperage is too low, the chimney cap wobbles, the dry wall between guest room and garage is not fireproof, the rain diverters are aimed right at your deck, the circuit breaker box cannot be installed over the Powder Room toilet, and you have an eight-foot sinkhole in the back yard.

Armed with a roll of plans, a leakless plumber, and an eight-foot sinkhole, we check the classifieds for furnished apartments.

A Puzzle Puzzle

A crime of monumental proportions was perpetrated in the Sunday, March 31 issue of *The Gazette*. The felony was so heinous, that the only suitable punishments for the evil deed-doer would be to lick peanut butter off the back of a porcupine, or spend a weekend as a guest of the Inquisition, or be strapped to a chair and forced to watch re-runs of the Martha Stewart Show twenty-four hours a day for a month.

The thousands of Beaufortonians who are dedicated, passionate, rabid puzzle-solving addicts spotted the crime at once.

The bottom section of *The New York Times* Crossword Puzzle was brutally chopped off. Oh, woe! Oh, misery! A Greek tragedy.

The clues were there. But no little boxes to write in the answers. Clues like "Salon specialist," "Make laugh," "Gutter site," "Not of the Cloth," and "Farmers Overalls" will forever go unsolved. Unrequited puzzle-lovers became victims of some cruel technical or human glitch.

It's OK to misspell Yasser Arafatz, refer to our President as George W. Push or report that Bluffton is really a suburb of Beaufort, N.C. We can live with these modest boo-boos, might even find reason to chuckle a bit.

But when the sacred *New York Times* Crossword Puzzle is mutilated, it causes psychic pain and suffering to those puzzle aficionados who, with a raised pen (if they're smug) or pencil (if they're humble) look forward to a few Sunday hours of intimate relations with The Puzzle.

So how did it happen? Vengeance, maybe. Are puzzle-solvers especially delinquent about paying subscription fees for home delivery? Maybe someone forgot to lock the office door one night and an evil stringer for a Savannah newspaper slipped in and sabotaged the puzzle.

A computer glitch? Always a good excuse—true or not.

Whatever the cause, there are now a slew of Beaufortonians in mourning, deprived of their delightful weekly frustration, bereft of the chance to test their wit and vocabulary, denied the exhilaration of near triumph as the little boxes get filled.

57

And even worse: their weekly "fix" has been denied. Without a puzzle to mainline, they may soon suffer profound withdrawal symptoms—like seeing snakes and beetles swarming in their box of Fruit Loops.

Save them, *Gazette*. Oh, save them!

A solution, perhaps. We'll keep the bottom of page 5D of the Focus section. You print the missing bottom third of the puzzle. When you do, we'll clip it out and scotch tape it to the upper third, being very scrupulous about lining up the boxes.

It'll give us puzzle nuts something to look forward to.

To live for.

Holy Smoke

It was an honest-to-goodness, down-home, glory-to-God, soul-and-spirit-purifying festival conducted by the righteous members of the First Pentecostal Holiness Church in Aiken.

The event might have been something right out of Adolph's fevered brain as he wrote *Mein Kampf*, or out of Mao's *Little Red Book* as he plotted to destroy Chinese culture.

There was the sign in big letters outside the church: Book Burning, Wednesday, 7 P.M.

The congregation was urged to cleanse their lives and homes of "inappropriate" literature and "whatever else has the appearance of evil" declared the Rev. R.K. Reeves. And burn it—as "a testimony before the Lord."

To minimize ambiguity, the congregation received a shopping list of bad, evil, corrupt, ungodly, impure, scatological, foul, contemptible items. They were bad things that might be luridly snickering from a bookshelf corner or slimily seductive while hidden under the mattress of a teenager.

While not exhaustive, items doomed to be incinerated included Harry Potter books, Pokemon items, adult magazines, R-rated videos, violent video games, and t-shirts that advocate popping a little Ecstacy or celebrate rock groups like Black Sabbath.

One lady member of the congregation allowed as she'd "feel better" as the flames from a 55-gallon drum devoured the evil stuff. "I feel dirty with it here, and…if you keep it in your home, it will finally get you."

Maybe the Rev. Mr. Reeves knew more about the tastes and reading habits of his flock than the flock realized. Maybe he knew about those soft porn videos at the back of the closet shelf, the adult magazines stuffed into a Hoover dust bag, or the Kiss t-shirt in a plastic bag down in the crawl space.

At least he had the decency not to encourage the wearing of loin cloths, the painting of faces, or frenetic dancing around the huge flaming barrel. The fire would hungrily devour the sins of the congregation, restoring them to a state of purity and innocence.

It's comforting, I suppose, to realize that some memorable and infamous traditions of the past have not been abandoned. It's been 70-odd years since the Nazi Party enjoyed joyous book roasts in town squares. And it's been some 40-odd years since Chairman Mao confiscated and/or destroyed literary and artistic works, consigning painters, poets, and pianists to hard labor on pig farms or tea factories.

With the first Church Book Burning a flaming success, can we expect that First Pentecostal Holiness will plan and carry out the next logical steps in its march toward unblemished sanctity?

Step One: burn evil stuff in a barrel. (Done.)

Step Two: selectively burn libraries that sully their shelves with erotic tales.

Step Three: burn down the homes of evil book/video/t-shirt buyers.

Step Four: tie dirty book and t-shirt buyers to a telephone pole and burn 'em.

Each of these four steps enjoys powerful historical precedent.

And why not?

Burning has always been easier than thinking.

Lettuce Be Patient

News Item: Airline industry to trim operating costs

The flight attendant looked serene, even a little saintly, as she struggled to maneuver the balky food cart up the aisle toward me. She stopped at my row, fixing me with a beatific smile.

"Tuna Salad Plate or Turkey Sandwich with Pasta, sir?" She made them both sound drenched in Olympian nectar. Encouraged by her inviting smile, I replied promptly, not wishing to jar the halo that seemed to hug her auburn hair.

"The tuna salad, please."

"With or without?"

With or without? I thought. *With or without what? Tuna Fish?*

"Uh…with or without…?" I ventured timidly.

"With or without lettuce, of course." Her smile was melting me.

"I'm sorry, miss…with or without lettuce….where? The tuna plate is really a sandwich?"

She tossed her auburn tresses impishly.

"No, sir. With or without a lettuce leaf under the scoop of tuna salad. You know…tuna is always nestled on a bed of lettuce. But on this airline, you have a choice!" Her smile widened, revealing Colgate teeth.

"Uh…excuse me, miss. I've been travelling for over seven hours. I've had four scotches. My right knee is throbbing. I'm not sure I'm ready to make a choice. Do I have to?"

"Not at all, sir. If you choose not to choose between with lettuce or without lettuce, you will receive a tuna salad plate without lettuce."

"I see…." I didn't see, really. But the lettuce option issue was beginning to assume a bizarre dimension, compelling me to ask: Why?

"Airline policy, sir." She tittered demurely. "Belt-tightening, you know. Our financial wizards discovered that the company could save one million dollars a year by eliminating the lettuce leaf from under the salad." She bent toward my left ear, whispering intimately:

"No lettuce, no pay cut. I'm sure you understand…."

"But I thought you said I could have the tuna salad plate with lettuce. Not violating airline policy? Not cutting your salary?"

61

"Not at all, sir." Her eyeballs rolled in discreet amusement. "I'll be delighted to slide a lettuce leaf under your tuna for a nominal extra charge of…"

"Extra charge??"

"…only fifty cents, sir. We now carry several heads of lettuce on every flight with tuna salad on the menu. To accommodate our passengers."

"Fifty cents!!"

Several passengers turned to look at me uneasily. A case of rage?

Regaining my control: "For one lettuce leaf?"

Her smile, I detected, began to decay slightly.

"Well, sir…it's…it's labor-intensive. We have to carefully remove one leaf from the head, trying not to damage it. Then we have to wash it. Then dry it thoroughly. You don't want soggy tuna, do you, sir?"

"How many passengers on this flight, miss?"

"One hundred thirty-six."

"How many agreed to pay fifty cents for a lettuce leaf?"

"I think about fifty-five, sir." A crease appeared between her eyes.

"That's…" I calculated furiously, "that's…$27.50. And you probably get at least ten leaves to a head…. Which means you need five and one-half heads of lettuce. Last I saw was that lettuce sold for sixty-nine cents a head…"

"Sixty-five cents at my supermarket, sir."

"…which means that you're collecting $27.50 for less than $4.00 worth of lettuce! The airline is making a profit of $23.50!"

"Well, there's the overhead, sir." The sparkle was now gone from her eyes.

Her lips tightened against those Colgate teeth. "With or without, sir." She made it sound like the last rites.

"Skip the tuna. I'll have the turkey sandwich."

"With or without the pickle, sir?"

Supermarket Follies

*A*n average day at your local grocery supermarket? Don't be fooled. A lot of dramas are unfolding all the time. Just take your nose out of your little human shopping list long enough to enjoy a few oddities in the behavior of fellow shoppers.

There is, for instance, the occasional shopper who will exhibit the Bobby Unser Syndrome. It's the cart-pusher who drives to excess speed in search of three items still missing from tonight's dinner menu, and who's got a wife illegally parked in the market's fire lane. He approaches the cross aisle at about 30 mph. If the cart had disc brakes, it would come to a screeching halt to avoid a collision with a family of four. The abrupt stop causes a twelve-pack of Pepsi to vibrate, tremble, then tumble onto a carton of Eggland Large. Several mumbled apologies are offered, but the eggs are now an omelet.

There's the SPA (Scrupulous Produce Assessor)—sometimes referred to as Fusspot. The shopper will slowly and methodically examine six heads of lettuce, peering suspiciously under each leaf, before rejecting all of them. Or will palpate, squeeze, and caress a dozen purple plums, then select two. Both will then be lovingly lowered in a plastic bag, as if each were a Star of India diamond. Then casually dropped into the cart from a height of about three feet.

Shopping excursions sometimes are, it appears, an excuse for convening a meeting of the Supermarket Friendship Circle. Two or three acquaintances, usually ladies—one each, maybe, from Seabrook, Fripp and Dataw—will circle their shopping carts like Conestoga Wagons to swap news of children, husbands, church, or the price of pork loins. Their conversation is lively, affable and newsy. They tend to convene, however, in the narrowest passage on the supermarket floor, effectively creating an impenetrable roadblock. Other customers will politely sigh and find an alternative route to dairy products. Other less polite shoppers will growl an "Uh...excuse me, Ladies!" Mildly chagrined, the Friendship Circle dissolves in different directions leaving behind a flurry of "ta-tas".

Having survived the speed demon, the fusspot or the chatty ladies, we'll encounter the Domestic Dilemma shoppers. Usually a husband and wife, they're parked, say, in front of the cat food shelves. There, they vigorously debate the variety, flavor, nutritional value, and cost of different brands. "You know Skippy hates anything with cheese." "But look, dear, the label says no cheese." "You know you can't always believe what it says on a label!" "But I'm wearing my glasses." "Check the lower shelf."

The debate, low key but serious, will continue for another ten to fifteen minutes. All the while, you're hovering impatiently on the fringe of the domestic tension, eager to grab a stack of Friskies Ocean Whitefish with Rice, and wondering what kind of spoiled and arrogant pussycat Skippy has become.

On rare occasions, we'll encounter the Haunted Seeker. You can spot this type of shopper by the darting eyes, furrowed brow, and rapid twisting of the head. It's the customer who desperately needs a very particular item—but can't find it. You can almost hear the fevered anxiety: "Red grapes! They moved the red grapes! They were right here only a week ago! Gotta have 'em for the salad or I'll die! Hey, produce guy, where'd you hide the red grapes?? Why are you doing this to me!"

But nothing is as dramatic as the Checkout Dash. There's something Olympian in the sudden appearance of three loaded shopping carts all driving toward the same unoccupied checkout station. All three cart pushers eye each other warily, wondering whether aggression or submission should prevail, whether politeness or rudeness will work. They move; they hesitate; they smile weakly at each other; they move again in unison. Will any of the three hesitate, weaken, withdraw from the combat? No matter. There's an announcement: "The register in aisle four is now open." Calamity avoided.

Really much more enjoyable watching people than picking potatoes.

Death of a Library

I t never pays to be smug.

Just when you're convinced that the very last pea-brained anthropoid had lumbered out of a dark cave into the radiance of humanoid enlightenment—oops, there's another one.

This one—his brainpan still swimming in primordial ooze—committed a most heinous crime against humanity.

He killed a library.

A man from Kentucky recently convinced his town council that building the first community library was a waste of tax dollars. And the town council—perhaps a few of his cave buddies—agreed and voted it down.

Good for you, you persuasive devil! You're a rock-ribbed, knee-jerking, no-frills, meat-and-potatoes kind of guy. You've got your primeval priorities in good order.

Who needs a library? After all, you announced that you've got your own library at home—the Bible, a set of encyclopedias, and "a few magazines." What else could your wife and three kids possibly need to be literate, productive, and civilized humans, eh? Who knows—maybe you're one of those zealous Bible-thumpers who believes that the Devil lurks in library stacks. Aren't libraries the place where an inquisitive kid can learn how to assemble an atomic device, find a plan for a zipgun, or gawk at nude Samoan women in the *National Geographic?*

Don't libraries harass their patrons by demanding they keep quiet, keep their feet off the reading tables, and pay fines? Even worse, don't libraries have books written by homosexuals? Chilling thoughts.

But having achieved this Pyrrhic victory, maybe you're ready to aim your tax-saving crusade at other tax-sucking town frivolities.

You get water from your own well, right? Who needs to support a treatment plant. And a septic tank? Great. You'd be a fool to pay sewer taxes. Never had a fire? Not a nickel for that new pumper the volunteer chief's been crying for. You've never pilfered so much as a ten-cent toy from the local K Mart—so who needs a Sheriff's Department?

And your three kids are done with public school, right? So what's all this foolishness about needing computers or more teachers? Hell, you made it through the eighth grade, and now pull down $800 a week making plastic bumper guards for cars without the help of any dang library.

Maybe if we could meet for a couple of Buds in your favorite local pub, I'd try—hopelessly, perhaps—to offer a gentle argument or two. For instance, when a community builds a school, it's saying that we recognize and honor the promise of the human mind and the hope for educated and effective citizens. When a community builds a hospital, it's saying that we recognize and respect the sacredness of the human body. When a community builds a church, it's saying that we recognize and revere the glory of a Deity.

And when a community builds a library, it's saying all that is past is prologue to the future. It's saying we're now the proud inheritors and beneficiaries of over 5,000 years of human achievements, ambitions, and ideas.

A library isn't books, it's beacons—a glow that guides citizens to the joy of learning, exploring, discovering, improving.

Maybe even finding a better way to make plastic bumper guards.

Clumsy Crime Caper

The Universal Manual for Felons and Other Miscreants (Fifth Edition, Annotated) identifies as Rule #1: "The successful thief shall have an IQ of at least 50."

This rule is often violated by assorted bandits, robbers, pilferers, larcenists, cat burglars, second story men, blackmailers, pickpockets and shoplifters—giving rise to the phenomenon known familiarly as the Dumb Crook Syndrome.

Recently, two novice felons, afflicted with this Syndrome, attempted back-to-back stick-ups at a pair of local businesses. Armed with a combined IQ of 37, a BB pistol, and an overdose of *chutzpah*, they hit an insurance agency at 8:00 in the morning and a loan company at 8:50.

That neither business normally keeps baskets of hundred dollar bills perched invitingly on a reception desk, and almost never conducts cash transactions, apparently eluded our felons, obliging them to settle for a couple of laptop computers, a wallet, and a purse.

The dumb duo had now violated Rule #2 of the Manual: "The successful thief shall have ascertained, in advance, the precise nature, volume, and location of cash, or other negotiable assets, prior to conducting a heist. In short, a thorough casing of the joint(s)."

To further compound the brain-challenged *modus operandi* of the pair, our untutored felons drove to their target in a stolen car. Not just a stolen car, mind you, but a *rented* stolen car—an act certain to incite the wrath of both the vehicle's lessor and lessee. The legal department of Hertz, Avis, or Enterprise has never expressed any charitable feelings toward dumb crooks who use one of their properties without first producing favorable reports from their parole officer, a clergyman, and their mothers.

Rule #3 was broken: "Never steal before you steal."

It would not have been surprising if the pair of larcenous dimwits had planned to hit a Day Care Center on Ribaut at 9:30 A.M. (Don't little kids bring lunch money?) But after brandishing the BB pistol and making a few growling noises, they'd have dashed out triumphantly with a haul of five Oreo cookies and a set of alphabet blocks.

Or a strike at 10:00 A.M. at the YMCA. (Don't health nuts leave wallets in their lockers?) The Y being another cashless venue, the dopey duo would have been forced to settle for three wet towels and a pamphlet on nutritional eating.

Even unloading the stolen car was classic ineptness. They dumped it where authorities quickly found it, thereby violating Rule #4: "Dispose of stolen vehicles by (a) repainting, (b) changing license plates, (c) torching, or (d) depositing in a deep body of water." They ignored the Rule, of course, allowing the Sheriff's men to spot it, complete with stolen booty in the back seat. (Rule #5: "Fence hot goods fast.")

The bizarre unraveling of this dumb crook caper provoked the Sheriff to say, "Something on the grits ain't gravy," a statement that should be sent promptly to language maven William Safire for his collection of unique and colorful Southern colloquialisms.

A veritable posse of some 30 well-armed law enforcement officers conducted a manhunt for the miscreants. They needn't have bothered. Given the cerebral deficiencies of the two felons, they probably would have tried to stick up the Sheriff's office.

All in all, we should be grateful to our dense duo. Crime doesn't often produce a gratifying giggle.

The Big Reward

What a deal for a virile Palestinian fellow!

The promise of receiving, upon dying as a hero, a trip to Paradise and the affectionate attentions of 72 virgins (or houris, as they're called) is surely a very attractive offer. It's a reward that's certain to steel the nerves of the suicide bomber and to suppress the thought of being fragmented into oblivion to earn a passport to Paradise.

Is it true that 72 virgins will welcome martyrs? As an article of faith in the present Islamic world, we're obliged to respect and accept the reality of the promise.

But as with any extraordinary offer, the candidate for martyrdom—as any Better Business Bureau will strongly recommend—is well advised to ask a few questions before flipping the switch and decimating himself.

As a service to the prospective suicide bomber, here are some sample questions:

—How did they come up with the number of virgins in the welcoming committee? Islamic scholars say there's nothing in the Koran ("Quran" to be correct) that promises 72 untouched, unsullied and voluptuous women. The Quran mentions "rivers of wine," but not six dozen sultry and seductive creatures.

—Is there any waiting period before the 72 luscious gals appear before the martyr? Are the virgins delivered all at once or spread out over several millennia? Does a visitation schedule have to be drafted? It could be a possible source of frustration for a guy who just went all to pieces.

—What sort of facilities will be provided in which to entertain and enjoy the attentions of the 72 ladies? A large tent strewn with soft pillows? Ivory bowls of succulent figs and sugared dates? A smoking water pipe to calm one's soul and recover one's vigor after a lively encounter with an especially energetic virgin? Environment is everything. It should be checked out.

—What if—unthinkable, perhaps—several of the 72 houris are overweight, have moustaches, arms as thick as ham hocks, or bunions on both feet? Does Paradise offer an exchange policy? There's really nothing appealing about being bear-hugged by a 315-pound virgin.

69

—Finally, consider the theory of hedonic contrast. If all 72 virgins are equally and inexpressibly beautiful, might you get bored? Any excess of exquisite looks can become tedious.

But what's the reward in Paradise for a teen-age *girl*, explosives strapped to her body, who joyfully deconstructs herself in a crowded restaurant? As a female with normal biological interests, what's she going to do with 72 female virgins? Maybe special provisions are made by the Imams in charge: 72 muscular, sensual and adorable male models?

And we hear that the age level for human dynamite sticks is lowering. Boys of ten, eleven or twelve now qualify for shredding their bodies at a crowded bus station. True, some twelve-year-olds can be sexually precocious—an anatomical rarity.

Imagine a ten-year-old arriving in Paradise and being engulfed, swarmed over and snuggled by 72 concupiscent virgins. But Paradise managers probably know what kids like: 72 Play Stations loaded with Atari Combat Two cartridges, all challenging them to demolish enemy tanks and hotel dining rooms.

These are all critical questions and issues. Candidates for Self-Destruct Seminars should check them out now.

Complaining isn't allowed in Paradise.

Part Three
The Arts

A Fine Idea

The quest is unending.

A strategy to find new sources of revenue—earned, unearned, borrowed, laundered, stolen—to support a community's cultural programs has become the grand obsession.

Not so for local and state government. They've found a neat, effective and simple way to generate revenues that help pay for good services.

Fines.

Hunters or fishermen who bag the wrong game or exceed the set limits pay hefty fines for their sins—money that's plowed back into environmental conservation programs to, say, re-stock fish hatcheries. Cash penalties imposed on intoxicated drivers support community educational programs that promote safe driving.

A great idea. Sin supports service.

Why arts agencies haven't yet adopted this concept escapes all reason. Lord knows the arts have their share of sinners, miscreants, and violators. Let's make 'em pay for their improper behavior as a way of supporting the programs they're sinning against.

Take a Beaufort Symphony Concert, for example. I offer below a Schedule of Fines that can be levied on concertgoers for unfriendly, unsocial or intemperate acts perpetrated before or during a concert.

Late arrival	$ 10.00
Late arrival, nasty to ushers	25.00
Carrying drink into hall	15.00
Carrying two drinks	22.50
Concealed tape recorder	50.00
Message beeper	5.00
Beeper activated	100.00
Coughing (up to 3 hacks)	10.00
Coughing, persistent	25.00
Crunching cough drops	15.00
Loud sucking of cough drops	50.00
Sneezing	5.00
Triple sneeze	15.00
Blowing nose (up to 5 seconds)	7.50

Blowing nose (over 5 seconds)	15.00
Yawning	5.00
Nodding off	15.00
Sleeping	30.00
Snoring	75.00
Audibly humming melody	50.00
Audibly humming, wrong key	250.00
Whispering	15.00
Talking aloud	50.00
Mildly intoxicated	5.00
Intoxicated, wobbly	15.00
Blasted	100.00
Applause between movements	150.00
Delayed "Bravos"	15.00
Weak "Bravos"	25.00
Leaving during loud passage	5.00
Leaving during soft passage	150.00
Sneaking out at intermission	250.00

A mechanism for collecting fines will need to be designed. Usher might roam the chamber with a collection basket attached to a long pole. Perhaps known offenders might pay their fines in advance or deposit a large amount with management as a "line of credit." Perhaps a cart—the kind airline shuttles use—might work the aisles accepting and imprinting credit cards. I'm sure it can be worked out.

If applied forthrightly and diligently, red ink will turn black. Sin will produce solvency.

It is, I think, a Fine idea.

The Magic of Goonkuk

A few hundred thousand years ago, a bunch of the boys returned from work one night, back to the big, dank cave under the craggy cliff they called home. They wore skins taken from the backs of animals, although you could hardly tell where the animal skins left off and their own hairy bodies began. They didn't talk much as a rule—just grunted a lot.

On one particular night, they were grunting with more enthusiasm than usual. In fact, they were grunting triumphantly. With their sticks, stones, and crude spears, they had brought down a saber-tooth tiger—a big bugger who must have given them an awesome battle. The boys were thrilled. They jumped around the fire, waved their spears in the air, and probably drank a lot of…whatever it was they drank a lot of in those days.

One of them suddenly got a bright idea. (And bright ideas—any ideas—weren't easy to come by back then.)

He picked up a piece of yellow stone, ran to the wall of the cave and started scraping the stone on it. A hush fell over the primitive crowd as they watched his oddball behavior. The boys scratched their hairy arms, legs, and faces trying to figure out what this skinny little guy named Goonkuk was doing. He'd never behaved like that before. Not Goonkuk, "the quiet one."

As they watched in silence, they realized that Goonkuk wasn't just making scratches—he was drawing lines. Some straight. Some curved. And the lines were beginning to take on a familiar shape.

The boys gasped—or at least they made grunts that sounded like gasps. They'd never seen anything like it.

Was this magic? What strange spirit was possessing Goonkuk?

A few more strokes—and there, right in front of them on the wall of the cave, was the tiger they killed that day. The very tiger! And right next to the tiger was another shape. Holy dinosaur! Was that Goonkuk himself, standing there with a spear in his hand?

The silence lasted a long time. In the frail light of their fire, the tribe stared at the strange scratches. But they weren't scratches any more. Not really.

It was different.

75

Goonkuk slid away to a dark corner of the cave, an odd smile on his face.

Slowly, one at a time (they were a little afraid, you see, of the weird magic that Goonkuk possessed), the hairy guys approached the wall and gradually worked up their courage to reach out and touch the tiger. Hands trembled. Was it real? It looked real. Would it leap off the wall and attack? Hands tightened around spears.

Slowly they turned and lumbered toward Goonkuk, their eyes wide, unblinking. As one, they dropped to their knees in front of him and pressed their foreheads into the cold earth of the cave floor. Goonkuk, they were convinced, was possessed of a strong spirit, an awesome power.

He could—with his own hand, with a piece of stone—create a tiger to help them remember the great battle, to recapture the terror and pride of the hunt, to remind them how brave they all were.

There was magic in Goonkuk. Magic in the yellow stone.

Goonkuk's tiny smile lingered. He had captured and preserved the moments of terror, of triumph, of pride. He had used his eye, his memory, his hand, his piece of yellow stone to share those moments with his world.

The artist was born.

Do the Arts Cause Cancer?

O f course they don't. And now that we're thinking about it, there are a lot of things that the arts don't do or cause.

Like wars. Fistfights, catcalls, and occasional high dudgeon, maybe; a critic slapped in the face with a kid glove; a hapless backer with homicidal feelings toward a bankrupt producer, perhaps. Things like that. An artist may record the blasphemy of war—a Goya, say—but he's never been known to start one.

Or like air pollution. It's rare to find a double bass violin or a slide trombone giving off noxious fumes. (Sounds, maybe, but not fumes.) Or dirty water. There may be a Sunday painter or two who might rinse the watercolors out of a brush in a bubbling mountain stream. But there have been no reports of cattle being poisoned at downstream watering holes.

And as for poverty—the baleful and ancient crippler of society— the arts are innocent. Considering the legendary image of the artist starving in his garret studio, or the actor lining up (yet again) for unemployment benefits, or the musician whose low wage constitutes a form of self-subsidy, we can certify that the artist spends more time escaping from poverty than creating it.

And the mountains of garbage that seem to be dominating the landscape. Not guilty. Critics have sometimes alluded unkindly to an exhibit of contemporary art as if it were solid waste, and certainly some stage performances have elicited olfactory comparisons. But the arts are simply not responsible for the dumping, shredding, or burning that befoul American communities. All too often, in fact, "junk" produced by some artists gets sold, unfortunately, and not burned.

The arts are not responsible for garish strip developments along our highways, or for monotonous housing tracts, or for sterile shopping centers. There are enough developers around to do that.

Or for the decline in church attendance, or the increase in the divorce rate, or the drop in faith in government, or the rise in the number of women and children beatings.

Yet for all their innocence, or perhaps because they work quietly and intensively to capture and preserve life, rather than damage or destroy it, the arts continue to be penalized by being assigned low priorities on economic and educational totem poles.

Maybe if we could, by some sneaky manipulation of scientific data, declare conclusively that egg tempera, greasepaint, or toe shoes were the causes of cancer, abandoned families, or the continental drift, more money would pour in from governments, corporations, and foundations.

Unhappily, the only mischief the arts cause is pleasure.

Little Roger's Tutu

I t's not hard to imagine the reaction of parents as their little Roger enters the room, toy stethoscope dangling from his neck, and announces, "I want to be a doctor!" Joy. Delight. Pride.

It's also not hard to imagine the reaction of parents as junior twirls in wearing skin-tight leotards, toe slippers slung over his shoulder, and announces: "I want to be a ballet dancer!" Horror. Embarrassment.

The kid needs a good beating, a good psychiatrist, or a good laxative. That sort of thing is acceptable for Susie. But for Roger? And if Roger persists, and his parents can swallow their humiliation enough to enroll the kid in a ballet school, Roger may find himself the only boy in the class.

Certainly one of the least logical and most pernicious of middle-class myths is the notion that any boy who wants to be a ballet dancer is almost automatically weird, queer or effeminate. The prejudice directed toward boys with a yen to become ballet dancers is about as rational as the old-fashioned prejudice toward girls with a yen to become neurosurgeons or astronauts.

Every ounce of historical, social, and anthropological evidence the world has produced demonstrates that a man's skill as a dancer is as much a part of his manly aptitudes as hunting, warring, or eating.

The Bible, for instance, is loaded with references to ancient priests, prophets, and peasants who expressed joy, sorrow, or religious zeal by dancing.

Try questioning the virility of a dancing African tribal chief. For an answer, you're likely to get a spear through your head. Or snicker audibly as a group of Native Americans perform a sacred rain or corn dance. They may not scalp you, but don't slow down long enough to find out.

And we don't have to reach back into ancient cultural tradition to illustrate the importance, relevance, or naturalness of the dance to men.

When we hear a sports commentator describe the "fancy footwork" or the "dancing around" prizefighters are performing, terpsichorean and pugilistic talents have merged. When we watch a slow motion version of a pro football team in action, we see leaps and turns and dips that would be the envy of the American Ballet Theatre Company. (A number of big college teams, as well as some of the pros, are actually given dance training to improve their speed, suppleness and precision on the playing field.)

Or watch a hockey player, or a skier, or people who fence and who depend on their dance-like nimbleness to keep themselves from being skewered.

Michael, Shaquille, and Alonzo are celebrated for (astronomical salaries aside) their great "moves."

There is scarcely a single rigorous sports activity that does not, at its very essence, demand the discipline, concentration, and intense muscular control of the dancer.

And even without practical applications, what's wrong about a guy who's able to move through life with a little poise, balance and grace? There are certainly too many slumpers, slouchers, and shufflers out there already.

Why are so many boys embarrassed by or reluctant to become professional dancers? Probably because we've all been brainwashed by the delicacy and frothiness—the prancing elves and flitting swans—of traditional classical ballet (forgetting that classical ballet is only one of many dance forms) and know little about the ferocious length and toughness of dance training.

You don't have to start preparing to become a doctor until you're in college. You have to start preparing to become a dancer when you're about 10.

So when little Roger begs you to let him be a dancer, say "no." Not because it may strike you as a silly, unnatural and unprofitable profession. But because he may not be able to survive the stiff discipline. It's about on a par with Marine Corps boot training.

But at the same time, please don't underestimate little Roger.

80

Never Too Late...For What?

If you're over 60, you're the target for every health and wellness drum-banger in the universe. "It's never too late," they urge breathlessly, to keep the body running on all cylinders; to revive sagging spirits and muscles; to preserve that sprightly step; and to re-capture, if not a Fountain of Youth, at least a Bubbling Brook of Maturity.

And their remedy for retarding or reversing the onus of aging? Walk, trot, jog, hike; bend, stretch, squat, climb; bicycle (moving or stationary), dance (round or square), swim (dog paddle or crawl); play tennis, play golf, play ping pong (but not Blackjack...too sedentary); skip salt, abandon fat, cut calories; walk the dog, chase the cat, enjoy sex (well, it's an activity). In short, do physical things and stop those arteries from getting rusted and crusted.

All very good. Vital, proven. Exercise and ye shall flourish. Great advice.

But the Stay Healthy cheerleaders of the world are focusing narrowly on physical activity, on the muscle structure of the neck, arms, shoulders, legs and heart. That's easy. They can show you pictures, x-rays, and medical studies to support their cause.

They are, however, focusing on only *half* the muscle that keeps seniors alive. They are telling us how to counteract the process of growing old; they are not telling us about the process of growing *up*.

That's where the other muscle comes in—the creative muscle, a sadly neglected part of the human organism. The creative muscle—an elusive phenomenon that resides in a person's mind, spirit and soul—contributes as much to the well-being, the feeling of self-worth, the sense of simply staying alive and vital as a two-mile daily walk.

The creative muscle is fueled by the imagination, by life-long experience, and by dreams—surely among the most precious assets of an older person.

The trick, however, is to translate those assets into action; to find the channel, the outlet, the catalyst for continuing to grow up; to begin feeding the stored-away appetite for reading, learning, dancing, playing a saxophone, capturing the lilacs in water colors, being a voice in the Hallelujah Chorus, photographing sunsets—discovering that the latent talent we all possess can come to life. What a way to transform declining years into arising years!

A healthy heartbeat is great. So is a healthy mind beat.

The arts are—have always been—an engine that drives the very human quest for personal fulfillment, for the exquisite satisfaction of mastering a new skill, a new language, a new way of communicating one's own value. And as good a motive as any for staying alive and healthy.

A Better Model

*C*an I prove it? Nope.

But I'm right.

High school kids who get into the arts—music, theatre, dance—are morally, socially and mentally more stable than kids who don't. And why? They're proud of the skills they possess and develop. They get recognition: applause as they take curtain calls at the end of a performance, a cheering crowd as their band sweeps down the field at halftime, hugs from family and friends after a dance recital. It makes each person feel like *somebody*. They bond to each other, knowing instinctively they need each other, that they must trust and protect each other—or the play, the band, or the dance falls apart.

They'll carry a saxophone, play scripts, or dance shoes to school—not a weapon.

With all the dire and deadly events in several schools lately, it was deliciously refreshing to learn about the eighteen-year-old Goose Creek senior who actually got to conduct the acclaimed Boston Pops Orchestra. Yes—up there on the podium, waving a baton at 80 of America's finest musicians.

Maybe you read about it. He learned via the Internet that for a contribution of a mere $10,000, the donor would be invited to stand before the orchestra, baton in hand, and lead them.

An impossible, out-of-reach, nutty dream, eh? How's an eighteen-year-old in Goose Creek going to come up with ten grand?

But he decided to try. After all, he was proficient in twelve (no less!) different musical instruments, his teachers and classmates had imbued him with a lot of confidence and self-esteem, and he wasn't afraid of work.

He took some eleven jobs—among them cutting grass, delivering pizzas, washing cars.

But he fell short. For all his enthusiasm, conviction and labor, the best he could earn was $5,000. Meekly, politely, he offered it to the Pops. And the Pops officials, having learned of the young man's passion and commitment, said, "OK—you're on."

So he conducted the world-famous orchestra in a rousing rendition of "Stars and Stripes Forever."

83

When it was over, the Pops management, recognizing an extraordinary kid, told him to keep the $5,000 and use it for college tuition.

The horrors at Columbine and Santee make headline, front page stuff.

The triumph of a talented Goose Creek high school musician—a stunning role model—should have also.

And with the lead: the baton is mightier than the gun.

A Few More Trophies, Please

T hose of us longish in the tooth will remember the words of a rousing tune of some decades past. "You Gotta be a Football Hero, To Get Along With the Beautiful Girls…"

Cute chicks may or may not be the reward today. But a star high school football player in the Lowcountry might get picked as the Athlete of the Week by the sports department of an area TV station.

And deserve it. Didn't "Leroy" slash, maraud, bulldoze his way through the opposing team for 150, 210, 273 yards last Saturday? Didn't "Samuel" leap, twirl and twist away from the frantically clutching hands of the enemy to set up the field goal attempt? And didn't the magic of "Roger's" awesome kicking toe save the spirit and honor of his school by five consecutive boomers through the goal posts? Wow!

Bravo! Huzzah! Bully! The camera crew arrives, the sports desk guy extends the trophy, "Leroy" (or "Samuel" or "Roger") smiles, stammers and thanks his parents, his coach, his teammates, his teachers, his God, and the manufacturer of his shoulder pads.

Now wouldn't it be novel and nice—as a matter of cultural equity and balance—if a TV station chose to recognize a different kind of hero. "Monique," for instance. She dances. In fact, she started studying dance when she was six, many years before "Leroy,"(or "Samuel" or "Roger") started hugging a pigskin.

She's endured a regimen of physical training only a fraction less punishing than a Marine Corps recruit. She's performed leading roles in "Nutcracker" and "Giselle." She maintains an A- scholastic average. And she's been selected to try out for the Junior Company of the American Ballet Theatre. And she's only sixteen.

To which TV station do we send nominations for Dancer of the Week?

And what about fifteen-year-old "Errol." Started tickling the ivories at age four. Passed off by several teachers who couldn't keep up with the velocity of his learning. He's mastered several Schubert and Beethoven sonatas, each containing over 1,000 notes—which stacks up pretty well against the 273 yards "Leroy" ran.

He's not afraid to noodle a little jazz on the side. Nice kid, balanced, not affected.

Which TV station will celebrate him as Young Musician of the Week?

And poor "Marco." He never gets any special attention except, of course, from his patient mother and his art teacher. Maybe that's because he makes weird objects out of wood scraps, strips of aluminum foil, plastic jugs, old battery jumper cables and broken Christmas ornaments—stuff most people ignore and throw away. But not "Marco." He's seventeen and will enter Savannah College of Art & Design on a full scholarship. The SCAD Dean doesn't think his "constructions" are weird at all. The Dean thinks he's a genius.

Suppose a TV station might offer a little statuette to "Marco," saluting him as Young Artist of the Week? (Maybe even ask "Marco" to design the trophy, if he can make it recognizable?)

Celebrating, encouraging and rewarding the brains, intensity, and physical power on the gridiron—or basketball court, or soccer field, or baseball diamond—is a fine service to athletics and to the public.

But where's the vehicle that recognizes and rewards the brains, intensity, and creative power of the community's outstanding young musicians, singers, actors, writers, painters, dancers? Where, in local or regional media, are a few Hosannas raised in their name?

Artists are heroes. They don't fight for first downs, or execute snazzy lay-ups. All they do is discover something beautiful in the world, and try to capture, preserve and share it.

Is Half a Kid Like Half a Loaf...

...better than none?

A lot of public school educators would seem to think so.

Because ignorance has never deterred me from reckless pontification, I'll remain consistent.

It is a fact, experts on the human brain tell us, that each side (hemisphere) of our gray matter performs different functions. The left lump, it seems, deals with practical things—like talking, adding up numbers, figuring the stress factor of bridges, clipping toenails, learning Spanish, knowing who's buried in Grant's Tomb.

The right side, on the other hand, is sort of impractical—like imagining, dreaming, creating, philosophizing, sensing patterns, shapes, sounds, speculating on infinite options, making quantum leaps.

With the left side, you can make a living; with the right side, you can relish living. The left side is control; the right side is freedom.

Simplistic? Not really. Where right brain skills have been woven into left brain school curricula, a little magic happens.

We're educating half the brain. Half the kid. And half a kid is worse than none.

If the medical establishment performed like the educational establishment, doctors would check only one eye, one ear, one lung. Dumb, huh? But in many classrooms, information is pumped into only one half the brain. The other half is told to go to sleep. And when music and art—primal residents of the right side—are axed from the curriculum (by left-brained people), or permitted only a token presence, we say to that half of the brain: die.

It's like saying that the capacity for finding creative solutions, seeing vivid connections, sharpening curiosity, exploring hidden pathways, or transforming hard reality into poetic imagery, are not germane to a well-educated person, to a civilized society.

If the search for both Truth and Beauty are still mankind's ultimate quest, then we'd better start talking and listening to both sides of a kid's brain.

If not, parents ought to demand a 50-percent rebate on their school taxes.

The Ancient Power in Kids

We still haven't figured out how to educate them; we don't know how to protect them from abuse; we offer them models and heroes who, in an eye blink, self-destruct from greed, stupidity, or powdery substances; we plunge them into a universe virtually paralyzed by conflicting ethical, moral and religious values.

Most criminal of all is that we blithely ignore, muzzle, stamp out, and sometimes even ridicule a kid's most precious, personal and inborn possession: the impulse—from deep in the genes—to cope with the world through the vehicle we call the arts.

Preposterous? Self-serving? Nope. Prove it to yourself.

Watch a group of kids—any kids, any age—hanging out together. Watch closely how they communicate with each other: they chant, they hum, they sing; they play-act other people, becoming other characters (TV hero, mother, teacher) through vocal changes, face-making, dialogue, pantomimic gesture—sometimes spinning out whole scenes. They leap, turn, bend, move rhythmically with their bodies while hand-clapping, foot-stamping, finger-snapping.

What we're seeing in the interchange among kids is a *Performance*—a veritable multi-arts performance that instinctively uses all the basic apparatus (however innocently) of the actor, singer, dancer, and mime. It's their natural second language. It's a way to co-exist, adapt, be funny, command attention, and shine in the eyes of their peers. No one taught them that. It's spontaneous and genetic, in the blood and psyches of kids.

And right from birth. Don't most parents use the arts, long before language develops, to "talk" to their kids, to stimulate them? They hang mobiles over the crib; introduce bright colors, forms, shapes; dance around with a child in their arms; play rhythm games; tell stories full of suspense, surprise, often by reading from books energized by vivid illustrations; and they sing, croon, hum to their kids.

In infancy, we give them all the tools of the arts; later, we take them away.

It's there in all kids—the seed planted centuries ago and transmitted across countless generations: the appetite to use shape and sound and

88

rhythm and bodily expression to give definition to their lives, to transform dramatic feeling into dramatic form.

It's a power, a reservoir. And sometimes I think the power scares us, and certainly confuses us.

Yet it's a power that can affirm the uniqueness, the identity of the child through self-realization. And it's drawn from the intuitive, inborn gift that is already there.

Arts the savior of kids? Probably.

After all, the entire school bureaucracy in this country is based on what we assume kids *don't* know—so they're obliged to attend school to learn it. And we're hearing that it doesn't always work.

What if education were based instead—centered around, emanating from—what kids *do* know: the power of music, the exhilaration of dance, the joy of impersonation and mime.

Ah…maybe society wouldn't fail quite so many kids.

We've Come a Long Way, Kiddies

My theatrical debut was overwhelmingly insignificant.

I played a postman in a sixth grade Christmas skit in 1942, delivering messages about Christ's birth to an assortment of elves, gnomes, reindeer, and good children. In retrospect, the skit was a piece of absurdist comedy, the recipients of the message being largely the children of Jewish immigrants. But Miss O'Brien, the teacher, saw nothing amusing in it, except when Sammy Cohen's antlers slid off his head.

The episode is remembered because it illustrates the essence of the cultural diet offered to public school children in the late 30s and early 40s. The occasional skit, a 30-minute weekly encounter with the recorded voice of symphony conductor Walter Damrosch exhorting us to love classical music, and sing-alongs of patriotic tunes during school assemblies, constituted the bulk of our exposure to the performing arts. It was bland, sterile, and unmoving.

It is no longer bland, sterile, and unmoving. In the years since I broke into show biz with my mail (pillowcase) pouch slung over my shoulder, a small revolution has taken place. Inside schoolrooms, as well as out, it's been recognized that children are bundles of creative energy, that they have powerful and innate appetites for the arts, that they more completely learn the 3 R's when the big A opens pathways to their minds, imaginations, and bodies, and that they are a great market for good cultural products.

The past 40 years saw children's theatre become respectable, thanks to the pioneering of playwrights Charlotte Chorpenning and Madge Miller; saw the arts sneak in by the side door of school curricula from K-12, with classes that range from pre-school finger-painting to high school courses in play production; saw the formation of professional acting companies dedicated exclusively to playing for kids; saw television discover young people via "Sesame Street;" saw the formation of "magnet schools" that draw together young people of like talents in the arts; saw state and federal agencies create programs, provide dollar support, and otherwise encourage the pumping of creative ideas toward children; saw psychiatrists, psychologists, and social workers achieve startling results when the arts have been used as tools to penetrate the special world of the disturbed or handicapped child; and saw professional, year-round resident companies and sponsors of children's entertainment become established in Atlanta; Seattle; Detroit; Washington, DC; Portland, Maine; Syracuse, NY; and elsewhere.

Anyone not hitched to the kid wagon these days has not come out of the caves.

The unsecret message of this revolution: deliver quality cultural products to kids who *already* possess the skill and perception to enjoy.

If we want high-class adults to run our world, give them high-class stuff when they're kids.

It makes a lot more sense than watching the antlers slide off Sammy Cohen's head.

The Rescue of Robert
(A True Story)

Mozart knew how to reach Robert better than anyone else.
By the time Robert was seventeen, he lifted weights to stay lean and muscular; his sense of humor ranged from subtle to raunchy; he was an honor roll student; and he enjoyed escargot and buffalo steak.

But Robert was diagnosed, when very young, as learning disabled. Uncommunicative, fearful of social contacts, and disruptive under stress, Robert was in danger of slipping into an interior twilight world from which there might be no return. The professionals—psychologists, psychiatrists, counselors, tutors, classroom teachers—tried to prevent his inward drift. So did his parents. Lifelines were thrown, strategies suggested, exercises carried out, medications proposed—all aimed at combating the sense of frustration, failure and disorder that were eroding his ego.

Then they tried an ancient remedy: a dose of the arts. He started taking piano lessons. A patient teacher and an explosive pupil slowly began to communicate with each other. The language—music—was a different language; it offered a special order, and it addressed a primal impulse not threatened by the demands of normal adults, educational bureaucracies, or medical conundrums. Slowly, the world widened: the teacher spoke patiently to the pupil, the pupil spoke to the piano, the composer spoke to them both, and all of them began to speak to the listener.

His piano playing improved. It never reached Carnegie Hall recital level, but it didn't matter. Music gave Robert the chance to "speak" with assurance, to reach tentatively back into the real world, to tackle other problems with a restored confidence.

Robert now holds a B.A. in History and French, an M.A. in International Studies, and MLS in Library Science. He's currently Director of an agency with a half million dollar budget and a staff of 32.

The rescue of Robert by the arts is, fortunately, becoming less unique. Back in the mid-70s, noted researcher B. H. Bragg established that a deaf child's sense of failure with written words can be overcome by creative drama; according to Irwin and McWilliams, children with cleft palates can improve their verbal and social skills through play-acting; mentally retarded children, Marie J. Neale found, significantly improved their speech and language skills through art programs.

It would be a dangerous oversimplification to say that music alone saved Robert, or that the arts are blessed panaceas for all children's disabilities.

But when I listened to Robert play the piano, I thought less about the arts as a decoration to life and more about the arts as a pathway to life.

I know. I was there.

Robert is not his real name. His real name is Dan.

Dan is my son.

Tap Dancing on Thin Ice

I t's no wonder they're sometimes viewed as dodos, blithering lambs, or artistic *kvetches*. No surprise that they're often sublimely exploitable and vulnerable. No shock when their naked innocence needs to be quickly and expensively protected by lawyers, insurance men, bookkeepers, and managers. The only thing remarkable about their naïve behavior is that they display it as if it were a Medal of Valor, an Emblem of Purity, a comfortable Crown of Thorns.

The "they" are graduates of the schools and academies that teach music, theater, dance and the visual arts—many of whom are pumped into the real world with enough chinks in their professional armor to make them look like slices of Swiss cheese.

What provokes this frothing began (of course) at home. A son spent four years at a reputable school of art learning about brushes, palettes, pigments, the legacy of the Masters, and that elusive play of light and shadow on the nude model which the novice painter struggles to capture. So far so good.

He can mix colors like a magician. With a few strokes of a charcoal stick, he can evoke an image of sylvan delight. His portrait of a younger brother resonates with the melancholy devouring the subject at the moment. Wonderful.

But for all its splendid and intensive training, the school never introduced him to a miter box so he could properly frame his pictures. They never troubled him with the issues of "artists' rights," "fair market value" of art works, commercial gallery operations, or otherwise coping with the world outside the academy cocoon with a weapon any mightier than a tube of Burnt Sienna.

And it's not just schools for painters or sculptors that behave more like monasteries than preparatory places. Serious students of music—vocal or instrumental—are often so engulfed by matters of pitch, cadence and tone, it's evidently considered immoral to ruffle them with banal matters of performance and recording rights, the role of music licensing agencies, dealing with agents and managers, the logistics of touring, or anything as pedestrian as artist contracts.

There are exceptions, of course. A few special programs have begun to surface that, without threatening the integrity of the art form, introduce the student musician, actor or painter to the fact that art is a business, a global industry, and fiercely competitive.

But real-world training remains sparse and flimsy in most academies, producing students who are marched into the industry jungle equipped with hardly more to protect them than toe shoes, palette knife, and dreams of glory.

I'm not proposing that artists—of whatever ilk or discipline—be obliged to become shrewd administrators, legal eagles, or CPAs. Being an artist is enough of a burden. But to dispense and receive a diploma without inhaling at least a whiff of real world imperatives—politics, business, law—is both unconscionable and hazardous.

It's like asking the artist to tap dance on thin ice.

Singing vs. Sweating

The clamorous guy at the other end of the bar was vociferously berating the Beaufort County school system. Public schools are, of course, tasty and easy targets for the disgruntled masses. This bar mate had, however, a very specific target in mind: the school chorus.

Why, he demanded scornfully, does his daughter receive credit for singing in the chorus? Credit for phys ed—a manly, competitive thing—was OK. But chorus? *Music?*

It was the classic knee-jerking of the philistine mentality—i.e., the arts are impractical frills and totally lack the *machismo* of sweaty gym socks and sneaks.

I began to wonder what living would be like if his thinking prevailed. Music a useless commodity, unworthy of any reward? I began to speculate on a world devoid of music. Imagine a wedding without hearing Mendelssohn's "Wedding March" or a high school graduation without Elgar's "Pomp and Circumstance," or the arrival of the President without "Hail to the Chief," or a Democratic Convention without "Happy Days are Here Again," or a New Year's Eve without "Auld Lang Syne."

Imagine a church service with no choir, a cocktail lounge with no pianist tinkling away in a corner, a karaoke night with nobody belting out tunes. Imagine symphony orchestras, jazz trios, rock bands—all silent, vanished. Imagine the music of Bach, Mozart, Beethoven, Hoagie Carmichael, Cole Porter, and Irving Berlin never being heard again.

Imagine not crooning a lullaby to ease your infant child into sleep.

The wonder, joy, thrill of music—gone. And think of the several million musicians who would be unemployed.

Too extreme, right? Wrong. Never happen, yes? No. (It did happen, in this century, during Communist China's Cultural Revolution, when fierce demagogues and philistines took control and virtually wiped out music—except for adoring songs to Chairman Mao.)

But back to my bar mate's daughter and the credit she earns, to her father's puzzlement and chagrin, for participating in frivolous choral singing.

If I'd thought that I could penetrate her dad's beer-induced distemper, I'd have argued that whatever credit the girl receives should be doubled; nay, tripled.

Why? Chorus is not just chorus. It's a whole bunch of disciplines.

—Chorus is Mathematics: notes have numerical value; rhythms are expressed in fractions (4/4, 3/4, 6/8); accurate counting is critical.

—Chorus is Physics: reverberation and reflection of sound; the decibel value of volume; acoustical properties of spaces and surfaces where the chorus will perform.

—Chorus is Anatomy: the operation of the lips, mouth, soft palate, vocal cords; the breathing mechanism, the vital capacity of the lungs.

—Chorus is Social Studies: every piece sung reflects the lifestyles, cultural values and history of the period in which it was written.

—Chorus is Personal Discipline: stern demands are imposed on chorus members who must trade off individuality for the sake and success of the whole. They must learn, study, think to acquire the command of the music and words. They must be unwaveringly obedient to the director.

—Chorus is Spiritual: the greatest musical compositions in Western history have been choral works written in praise of God. (Suppose Bach, Vivaldi, or Mozart would deny credit for chorus?)

There's an irony that obviously escaped my bar mate. Long after the kids have forgotten what they learned in biology, history, English or French; long after their bones and muscles rob them of competitive sports—they still have music. They will listen to it, dance to it, get married to it, pray to God to it, ride an elevator to it, shop to it, march to it, be buried to it. And—who knows?—some may even make a decent living out of it.

Credit for chorus? Absolutely. In fact, it should be mandatory. For all students.

Puppet Power

The nine-year-old black boy doesn't know it, but he's playing God. With wood tongue depressors, string, scraps of cardboard, an empty Bird's Eye juice container, and Borden's glue, he is assembling a creature—creating out of simple materials an object that is slowly assuming the shape of a human being. Intently, he hinges the left arm to the shoulders with string. Now both arms are attached and dangle wobblingly. The head, a crude disc of paper, is still featureless, a blank façade awaiting the few strokes that will give it humanness. The boy holds his unfinished miracle up to the light, which produces on the wall behind him...

...shadows...of a thousand years ago...looming, weaving, vanishing...dancing on a silk wall to the beat of cymbals and incantations...Shapes of gods, demons, kings and beautiful queens reenact great battles and epic romances—dramas more ancient than the wizened men who cause the puppet shapes to move at the end of long sticks. The Royal Thai audience is awed by the magic of the shapes, by the passions they evoke, by the gods who make such miracles possible...

But he is interrupted by a classmate, a girl two years older and three years meaner. "You got no face, dummy! No eyes, no mouth—nothin'!" The boy reacts swiftly, with an instinct as primal as his genes. His wobbly unfinished creature rises to the defense, rushes into the face of the mean girl, and with a courage its creator has never known, shouts in a super ogre's voice: "I will chop you up and eat you for breakfast, you dirty snake!" The girl's puppet replies by butting its head into the wobbly miracle, which sends it...

...sprawling! To a hundred years ago. The crowd shouts with glee. "Get up, Punch! Get up, you rogue! You won't let a woman treat you like that, will you?" Punch scrambles to his feet, miraculously producing a large club. Judy, with a squeal that delights the farmers, blacksmiths and wheelwrights of the British village, begs for mercy. But too late. Punch swings, misses Judy, but strikes the passing Constable. The crowd, seeing the Law get whacked, roars its approval. Punch sulks...

98

...and returns to his crayons and paint to create flesh, color, eyes and mouth. In a few minutes, it's finished. The inert creature now waits for the passions of its creator to infuse life, voice, movement. The boy stares at it—at its listless eyes, its unkempt hair, its mottled black face. Suddenly, the boy hurls it to the floor, steps on it, crushing and dismembering it. He runs from the room...

...crying. Today in the Boston clinic, that's not unusual. Here most of the children cry or are eerily silent. Except, that is, when a sock with a funny face is slipped over their fists. And through the protective alter ego of their cotton friend, they will sometimes vent the darkness and fears that cloud the mind.

Puppets are magic. They can conjure spirits. They invoke and open other worlds—most of which are trapped inside us.

Clever Cousin Lester

My cousin Lester ("the famous eye doctor," his doting mother would endlessly proclaim) decided, at age 52, to play the cello.

He'd never had a shred of musical training prior to that decision, or even talked about it. He came home one day with a cello under his arm and an appointment with a teacher. His mother was distressed. "Music? What for? You're a famous eye doctor. And at your age!" Music study, she insisted, was for kids.

Lester produced one of his soft, enigmatic smiles and assured his mother that he was neither adolescent nor senile. He proceeded with the lessons, applying the dexterity of a surgeon's fingers to the cello strings. A few years later, he was creating the lush, resonant sounds so characteristic of that instrument. His mother never did understand her son's mad impulse for "playing a big fiddle."

But Lester understood. He knew that his antiseptic career as an eye surgeon filled only half of his spiritual cup. There was a vacancy in his life, a longing not only to repair, but to create. He could deftly pierce the human eye with laser blasts, but he could not penetrate the human heart with beautiful sounds. The cello was for him an emotional scalpel, an instrument for cutting through the blandness and routine of everyday existence and exposing the heart.

Lester is about 85 now. He's still playing the cello, joining other musicians in living room recitals, and is happy as a clam. (His wife, not to be outdone, and in self-defense, started taking piano lessons at age 55.)

Lester has never received an invitation to perform at Carnegie Hall, but that doesn't bother him. He's already found his greatest audience, his most satisfied listener, his most severe critic—himself.

There are lots of Lesters in this world—people who carry into older age the baggage of unfulfilled appetites, vague disappointments, frustrated desires for creative release they never had the chance to satisfy.

The arts, happily, are immune to age. They are forever young, endowing the person who enjoys them with a creative satisfaction and joy akin to youthful discovery. They won't reverse the aging process; they will enrich the living process.

My cousin Lester was smart. Despite his mother.

Skip the Valium

Need a breather from oppressive thoughts about the Middle East, taxes, mass killings, banana republics, and the horrors of child molesting? Simple.

Attend a performance of *Aida*. Need to get away from acid rain, nagging children, potholes and the bombing of embassies? Easy. Go see *Swan Lake*.

The notion persists, like a carbuncle on our culture, that the prime function of the arts is to help us escape, forget, find temporary respite from the disorder, lunacy, and general gloom of the real world.

The notion is not without merit, as producers of Broadway musicals will happily testify, along with other purveyors of entertaining glitz.

But the notion of art-as-escape, as a quick dip in the River Lethe, compromises the arts by being woefully narrow. It's like playing "Chopsticks" to demonstrate the full power of the keyboard. Clearly, something is missing:

—Art is not an escape; it is a reentry into the real and demanding world of myth, sound, color, and form—a world as ancient and as kaleidoscopic as the human race;

—Art is not an anesthetic; it is a stimulant to remind us that we are sentient creatures with a genetic appetite to respond deeply to creative images and symbols;

—Art is not a quick fix or a steam valve on our emotional boilers; it is an enduring reminder that we can indeed behave like a civilized race, and that we are ready to embrace anyone—and especially an artist—who will prove it;

—And art is not designed to show how weak we are in handling real world crises; it's designed to show that we have the strength, resilience, and emotional resonance needed to confront crises with more than a little bravery.

The arts, in sum, are not temporary analgesics like Super Strength Excedrin, Valium, or double Scotches. The pain usually comes back.

What the arts give us ultimately is the chance to balance reason against madness, beauty against corruption, and joy against despair.

And in the preservation of this awesome balance lies whatever future we may have as a humane society.

Part Four
Entertainment

Aliens Among Us

P lease, FBI, don't trash the X-Files. Passionate Agent Mulder and clinical Agent Scully have at last been vindicated. The truth is definitely out there—and now definitely here. Alien forces have landed, taken up residence on our helpless planet, and have now paraded their conquest on national TV.

I'm referring, of course, to the Billboard Music Awards that aired in December. If what we saw and heard is an omen for the new millennium, I'm for setting the date back to 1900.

The aliens, it seems, pay reverence to their own pantheon of deities: the God Rap, the God Rock, the God Grunge, the God—known only by its initials—R & B, and the God Hip-Hop, suggesting that an unusual species of bunny exists somewhere out in the cosmos. These are stern Gods who demand bizarre rituals, speaking in tongues, and the howling of eerie incantations.

Many of the aliens seem to sing through their noses, having perfected the technique of smelling a song rather than singing it. Their extraterrestrial music, in deference to their stingy Gods, usually consists of three notes which, like a *mantra*, are interminably repeated. This induces a trance-like paroxysm of mind-numbing bliss—probably not unlike chewing peyote leaves.

They also seem to consider a microphone a gastronomical delight, thrusting it deeply into their mouths until it rests just an inch or two above the large intestines.

It's the words, however, that most betray their alien origin. To the ears of us earthlings, the words are incomprehensible, consisting of gargled sounds that are evidently drenched in etymological meaning characteristic—or so the Hubbell spacecraft will verify—of the Planet Zog. Zog is located, unless my astronomical knowledge of deep space fails me, in the Fifteenth Quadrant of the Constellation Esophagus. How could anyone not be moved by "ahgonnayu," "diglickpah," or "skidlochem"—words that on Zog transform women into puddles of passion.

These luminous lyrics are even more powerful when enhanced by the atmospheric phenomena that the aliens use on their own planet. Saber-like slashes of brilliantly colored light lacerate the stage like the

105

laser swords in Star Wars. Smoke billows, spreads, and engulfs the aliens, turning them into spectral figures that twist, jerk, prance, jump, whirl, stomp, skitter, leap—clearly an example of the sacred ritual performed on Zog to celebrate the annual arrival of sand gnats.

Many of the aliens wear black capes—a tribute, no doubt, to Bela Lugosi, one of their earth idols.

For all their bizarre flamboyance, their howling of garbled lyrics, their three-note music, and their tribal gyrations, the aliens are a clever race. Their invasion was well-planned; where better to slyly insinuate themselves into the heartland of Earth culture than through the pop music industry?

It's a perfect cover.

The Bowling Show

I t wasn't guns or bombs that threatened my safety at age thirteen. It was bowling pins. Crammed into a tiny, poorly lit space at the back end of the alley, I was being paid 50 cents an hour to reset the pins—unless, of course, I was knocked unconscious by a flying, spinning pin that seemed determined to crack my skull. (When my mother discovered my working conditions, my career as a pin-setter was abruptly terminated. I didn't argue.)

I never bowled—income, back then, was more important than recreation. I never even saw the people who rolled the three little, holeless balls at the duck pins. Who cared? I was too busy covering my head and face with my arms.

Those were the days, of course, before AMF installed the automated pin-setting and score-announcing equipment now common in most bowling alleys, thus freeing thirteen-year-olds from bowling pin bondage.

It was when my wife was persuaded to join the VIP Seniors bowling team that I finally had the chance to actually watch bowlers in action, hurling their ten, twelve or fifteen-pound, three-hole balls at those coldly waiting and usually defiant pins.

It's been said that the way people play games reveals personality. That's certainly true of bowling. After extensive but totally unscientific observation, I discovered that bowlers fall into distinct *personae*, unique personality categories, a phenomenon that would have totally escaped my thirteen-year-old mentality.

Here's a partial catalog:

The Mafioso releases the ball, glaring at it murderously as it rolls toward the pins, clenched fist on hips, ready to put out a contract on the ball, the pins, the bowling establishment, the City and the County if the ball fails to demolish all ten pins.

The Cheerleader hurls the ball and immediately performs a series of spastic gyrations, hands furiously sawing the air, crouching, jumping, reminiscent of Margaret Mead's description of fertility ceremonies in Samoa.

The Greek Statue fires off the ball in perfect PBA form, one leg raised and bent behind the other, body leaning forward, the arm that

107

lofted the ball raised and frozen in position, in a pose that reminds one of the classical statue of Hermes poised for flight.

The Traffic Cop who, when the ball is thrown, the head, shoulders, torso, hands, arms, hips and feet begin a desperate body language communication with the ball, in the vain hope of altering its path and directing it toward glory.

The Shrieker who, when making a strike, a spare, knocking down any pins at all, or even rolling a gutter ball, produces an ear-splitting howl of joy or despair guaranteed to unnerve a bowler eight lanes away, or trigger an EMS squad race to the rescue.

The Hypochondriac succeeds in barely knocking down the seven-pin, blaming the bad roll on a strangely recurring shoulder pain, a sore thumb, a recent tooth extraction, or an unexpected twinge in the lower lumbar region.

The Aristocrat, so sublimely confident in his or her mastery of bowling technique and skill, turns his back on the pins the moment the ball leaves the hand, and saunters back to a chair. It is enough for the aristocrat to merely *hear* the ball collide with the pins, and has the dignity to ignore it.

Finally, *Pollyanna,* whose ball rolls cruelly into the gutter about a third of the way down the lane, but who, with hope that springeth eternal, stares at its failed path, imagining the ball will spring out of the gutter and topple all the pins.

This is hardly an exhaustive list of bowling character types—there being many subtle variations.

And to think I never got to watch the show when I was thirteen.

The New Millenium
Movie Rating System

P altry. Totally inadequate and obsolete.
The present Hollywood rating system is so obsessed with guiding the moral pathway of film-goers, you'd think it was a direct linear descendent of the Inquisition, or at least some dusty echoes of the old Blue Laws of Boston.

OK, it's not as bad as its predecessor, the notorious Hays Office—that banged the ethical gong when Clark Gable dared to take off his shirt in front of Claudette Colbert—but still dedicated to sharing with the movie-going public its estimate of a film's purity, vulgarity, or bloodiness.

The Rating System—the Gs, PGs, and Rs (nudity, sex, violence) is an injustice to both filmmakers and filmgoers. It's too limiting, too flimsy, too narrowly focused; it concentrates on the content of a movie, not its quality, character, style.

To remedy this baleful situation, herewith is offered a modest proposal for a New and Expanded Millennium Rating System, one that better prepares us for the experience of a movie, rather than merely warning us that our fifteen-year-old will be corrupted by seeing what he knew when he was twelve.

The New Millennium Rating System

"A" Rating: Arcane. Esoteric and abstract in the extreme. Ph.D. from Harvard, Yale or Texas A&M useful to even understand the title.

"B" Rating: Boring. Recommended for sleep-deprived. Faster-acting than Sominex.

"C" Rating: Couth. Polished. Civilized. Squeaky clean. OK to bring your maiden aunt.

"D" Rating: Depraved. Admission limited to child molesters, serial killers, and IRS agents.

"E" Rating: Erotic. Suitable for children under five, who will think it's funny, and adults over 70—who will think it's funny.

"F" Rating: Feminist. Macho guys stay home.

"G" Rating: Gory. Bring airsick bags.

"H" Rating: Holy. A merry mix of Old and New Testament stories. The bearded fellow will resemble Charlton Heston.

"I" Rating: Imbroglio. Utterly confusing. Plot synopses and road map dispensed by ticket-taker.

"J" Rating: Junkie. Yet another excursion into the dark underbelly of narcotics. Lots of dogs smelling laptops.

"K" Rating: Kraketoan. Disaster epic. Erupting volcanoes, meteors plummeting toward Fresno, Will Smith saving everybody.

"L" Rating: Lackluster. Zero tension. Suitable for persons with heart condition, asthma and acid reflux.

"M" Rating: Maudlin. Foolishly sentimental. Sobs and tears. Three hankies with each ticket.

"N" Rating: Nadir. The absolute pits. Lacks focus, style, clarity, humor, drama, point of view, credibility. Demand a refund.

"O" Rating: Obfuscate. See "Nadir."

"P" Rating: Predictable. Boy gets girl, boy loses girl, boy gets girl—all quite clear in first ten minutes.

"Q" Rating: Quixotic. Extremely romantic. Screenplays by Barbara Cartland clones. Candles and scented boudoirs.

"R" Rating: Remake. You saw this one in 1922, 1941, 1958, 1971, and 1984.

"S" Rating: Sleeper. No hype, no promos, no big stars—but you'll love it.

"T" Rating: Terrifying. A hair-curler, blood-freezer, gut-wrencher. Incontinence may occur.

"U" Rating: Uplifting. For persons in state of deep depression over lost love, lost job or lost law suit against IBM for copyright infringement.

"V" Rating: Vestibule. Where you should sit during this film, enjoying the over-priced popcorn.

"W" Rating: Whoa! Pray for a power failure, incompetent projectionist, or evacuation notice. Yes, that bad.

"X" Rating: XL. A film of epic proportions, running anywhere from 120 minutes to the length of a Martian winter.

"Y" Rating: Yang. For lovers of Stallone, Segal, Schwartzenegger. An effusion of rampant male hormones spewing into audience.

"Z" Rating: Zaftig. For devotees of *Sports Illustrated* swim suit annual. More pulchritude than plot. Yes, they're wearing swim suits, sort of.

And there it is. As a lover of the cinema arts and a public-spirited citizen, I joyfully assign all rights to this New Millennium Rating System to the Lords and Ladies of Hollywood. A grateful public will surely fatten their weekly box office grosses.

Assuming the public remembers the alphabet.

Try a Little Propylparaben

My singular achievement in using a chemistry set I got as a kid was to produce an obnoxious smell. The putrid aroma produced an irate parent, especially when it slopped a bit over some potatoes about to be peeled for supper. It left me with a lifelong distaste for the chemical sciences.

I wish it had been otherwise. I would then have enjoyed an appreciation for the miracles that chemical substances create in restoring silky skin, lustrous hair, and irresistible sensuality to adults questing for the Fountain of Youth.

When wrinkles make a face look like a plowed field, when the sacs under the eyes start to resemble backpacks, and when the skin takes on the character of an elephant's hind quarters—chemistry to the rescue!

The quest for eternal—or at least slightly prolonged—youth is hardly new. Men and women have been painting, rubbing on, or otherwise slathering themselves in weird concoctions for as long as human vanity has existed—like around back in the Pleistocene Era.

But now the Fountain of Youth has been replaced by the Formula of Youth—chemical preparations that purport to slow, if not reverse, the sometimes unflattering erosions of aging. Just read what those magic potions contain.

Is your skin dry, flaky, and looking like a riverbed after a thousand-year drought? Can you use your knuckles to sand down the rough edges of a birdhouse your kid made? No problem. Generously apply some mineral oil heavily laced with Triethanolamine, a squirt of Dioctyl Sodium Sulfosuccinate, a smidgen of PEG-40 Steanate, and a dab of Quarternium-15. Very therapeutic, and guaranteed, more or less, to restore luster and shimmer to your epidermis. Says so on the bottle.

And how about your hair? Does it have the texture of a whiskbroom, the sheen of a burlap bag, the styling of a wire-haired Terrier? Salvation's at hand. There's a product inviting you to lather up with Sodium Chloride, massage in a dollop of Methylisothiazinone, and sweeten the process with Extracts of Nettles, Hops, Chamomile, Henna, Rosemary and Horsetail. A combination of ingredients reminiscent of what the Three Witches in *Macbeth* might have whipped up.

And if the deep pores in your facial tissue beg for some deep cleaning, there's a product boasting a lively chemical assortment that includes Cocamidapropyl Betaine, Arachidomic Acid, Humus Lupulus, Coenzyme B5, B6, B12, Folate, Nicotrate, Q6-10, Riboflavin and Thiamine. And for good measure, a spot or two of Silicone, Magnesium, Copper, Iron and Zinc Ferment.

A hand lotion my wife uses has no less than 40 chemical compounds—most of which are both unpronounceable and inexplicable to the easily befuddled layperson.

There is, however, one component of these beauty, health, and ego-restoring formulae that is not strange. Water. I can say "water."

I even know what it is.

Hooked

Yes, I'm a user. A heavy user.

No power on Earth, in Heaven or in Hell could make me abandon my addiction to crossword puzzles.

As a dedicated, long-term puzzle freak, I've learned to think and write in puzzle-ese, the answers to clues having become part of my personal vocabulary. The next paragraph displays my bravura command of words learned from my passionate proclivity for puzzles.

The scene: Two tatars were sitting in a proa tied to an areca watching a lerot skitter. They were pouring twanky from a cachepot while discussing harmartiology. One was a capo with a box of methytrinitrobenzene on his lap. The other, plucking a sitar, watched a pangolin wander by and a pongid in a tree. The capo reached out to pluck an umbral that was covered with dors. He said, "I don't wish to seem anile or mono-maniacal, but I crave some matelote with some barbecued anoa." "I am eudemonic," said his friend.

Translation (for the uninitiated): Two mongol tribesmen were sitting in a small boat tied to a betel palm tree watching a small mouse skitter. They were pouring tea from an urn while discussing the wages of sin. One was a chief with a box of TNT on his lap. The other, plucking a Hindu stringed instrument, watched a scaly ant-eating animal lumber by and an ape in a tree. The chief reached out and picked a milkweed bloom that was covered with beetles. He said, "I don't wish to seem old-womanish or single-minded, but I crave some fish stew with some barbecued Celebes ox." "I'm happy," said his friend.

My father's to blame for my obsession with crosswords. Every night after dinner, he'd tuck a section of the evening paper under his arm, take a small, pocket-size red notebook out of the phone table drawer, and remove himself to the bathroom. The notebook, I later discovered, was his homemade crossword puzzle dictionary, a compilation of clues and answers he'd gleaned from doing puzzles over the years. Merriam Webster hadn't yet published its 767-page Crossword Puzzle Dictionary, so he had to concoct his own. I think I still have the little red book, although (disloyally) I also bought the Merriam Webster tome.

114

The blessings of being a puzzle devotee are many. I'm calmed and comforted during the sometimes interminable waits at a doctor's office, a car repair garage, or while the wife primps for going out.

It gives my conversation at cocktail parties a certain panache when I cheerfully inform other guests that a Dik-Dik is a kind of African antelope. Or if I should want some butter at a New Delhi hotel, I confidently request some ghee for my toast.

My musical friends are awed when I inform them that Guido's Highest Note is the simple three-letter ela. And no lecturer on art could baffle me by a reference to an Orozco work. It's a mural, of course.

I've just about mastered *The New York Times* Sunday puzzles. But it's *The London Times* that keeps me humble. Its clues are maddeningly adumbrate, numinous and orphic. For instance, one of its recent clues was the stumper "syllogistic confluence." Holding a Ph.D. from Oxford would probably help. Or an etymological brother.

I'll stick with Dik-Dik and Pangolin.

Fictional Fitness

I don't know where he got it, or whom he got it from. Certainly not from me—his sybaritic, indolent, Devil Dog-eating daddy.

He—my son, that is—is blessed with a lean, taut, muscular physique. If there's an ounce of fat on his body, it was dripped on him by a careless waiter. He's at a gym every day at 5:30 A.M.—yes, every morning, seven days a week. (His chief criterion for accepting a new job: a Gold's Gym within a ten-mile radius.) He's a Certified Personal Trainer who grows his own bean sprouts in little pots at his kitchen window. He sprinkles the sprouts liberally on his favorite dish; a kind of eerie goulash of exotic veggies and wheat germ, an alien-looking concoction that less dedicated fitness freaks might confuse with garden fertilizer.

His obsession with physical fitness, however, has inspired me to begin taking special note of what actions I perform regularly to achieve that Mr. Atlas look; to acquire agility, strength, and endurance. And without much effort, I discovered that I'm not doing too badly—even without membership at the Y, without a personal trainer, and without a stationary bicycle, rowing machine, treadmill, Nordic Track, or any of the other torture devices invented by the Inquisition.

For instance, I WALK regularly, all the way from the living room to the icemaker in the fridge to add a few cubes to my Pepsi. I find I must JOG my memory quite often, especially to recall where I hid the Hershey Candy Kisses. After several evening cocktails, I RUN with great determination to the john. I faithfully STRETCH the truth; that is, usually when asked why a full container of Planter's Deluxe Nut Mix is almost empty.

Every morning (God willing) I SIT-UP in bed, taking keen pleasure in how my abdominal muscles are being squeezed and tightened, followed by TOUCHING MY TOES to the floor. I TURN, REACH, and BEND in the shower, suffering this demanding fitness ritual with heroic glee.

At least twice a week, I CLIMB a flight of stairs to my computer, at which, with NIMBLE fingers, I access recent messages, usually an assortment of raunchy jokes E-mailed from as far away as the north of France. Groans and giggles, I hear, are great for my ABS.

The stress produced by all these challenging exercises is both exhilarating and exhausting. Invariably, it arouses the appetite.

That's OK. When it happens, I TROT to the kitchen, PULL open the fridge door, TWIST a carton to pour some milk, and TEAR APART the wrapper of a Devil Dog.

Just wait'll my son sees me.

Back to the Romans

Not all athletes are bent on crushing, creaming, clawing, clubbing, annihilating, trashing, clobbering, slaughtering, pulverizing or decapitating their opponents. But you wouldn't know it from the names of some teams or the headlines sports editors write.

For instance, fencers salute each other with their rapiers or epees before the parrying and lunging begin. Japanese wrestlers and karate combatants bow to each other before and after a match as a gesture of respect for the opponent. A winning tennis player will rush to the net to shake hands with the loser or, if agile enough, leap over the net. Opposing rugby teams will join together at a nearby pub to hoist a few dark brews in celebration or commiseration. Bowlers will offer a comradely high-five to an opposing team member who rolls a triple strike Turkey.

On the darker less gentlemanly side, Little League Dads (and Moms, sometimes) will assault an umpire or another parent if a call goes against their kid. Soccer fans, insanely protective of national pride, will storm the field and each other if their favorites lose. Auto racing devotees, mostly dormant while the cars scream around the track, become electrified by a crash, leap to the feet with arms flailing, and roar with excitement and delight, even as the ambulance and fire truck speed to the crushed car.

Pro and amateur sports, it seems, have become less a game and more a combat; less a healthy competition and more a collision of enemy forces. At times, the sports scene has a jungle quality, a savage place inhabited by goring bulls, swooping hawks, snarling grizzlies, vicious raptors, stalking panthers and voracious sharks.

Maybe as pro sports teams proliferate, as league rosters expand, as the battle for paying fans and gargantuan TV fees intensify, gore gets substituted for glory. To hype their product and tantalize the masses, teams adopt names that make a fetish out of ferocity, a virtue out of violence. Labels like Grizzlies, Wildcats, Hornets, Hurricanes, Avalanche, and Thrashers promise how the athletes will behave on the field.

The now-defunct XFL football league raised the promise of aggression and terror to new levels: NY/NJ Hitmen, Chicago Enforcers, Or-

118

lando Rage, Memphis Maniax, and Las Vegas Outlaws. Almost hinting at blood sport, the names are reminiscent of the halcyon days of Roman arenas.

Not to be outdone, sports editors catch the spirit and headline game results with sadistic delight: "HHP *crushes* BA boys," "Maryland *tears down* Wake Forest," "Devils *pound* Bruins," "Carolina *thrashes* Atlanta," "Hawks *slay* Dragons," "Tigers *claw* Southern," "Raptors *rip up* Knicks," and "Stars *disable* Sabres."

Can we look forward to such journalistic blood lust as: "Harvard *mutilates* Yale," "Hoyas *eviscerate* Blue Devils," or "Bulls *emasculate* Hornets?" That'll draw the crowds.

Maybe we'll tire of crushing, pounding, or slaying. Maybe we'll rediscover that there is, after all, a fundamental dignity, decorum and civility to athletic competition.

It'll probably never happen, but it might signal a sea change in the violent appetite of American sports consumers if teams appeared with names like Louisville Lovers, Boise BonBons or Pasadena Pussycats.

Think so?

Naw.

With Guitar and Nasal Twang

It would be awful if they were lost and forgotten.

Song titles, that is—especially the titles of Country Western songs that never made the big time or won a CMA award.

Soulful, gritty, homespun, funny, and sometimes quite religious, the titles were collected by Mike Harden of the Scripps Howard News Service about a dozen years ago. He named his "unabridged official" list "The All Time Best of the Worst Country Song Titles Ever." They're worth sharing, if only to preserve them.

The really weird thing about the song titles is that they're real. You couldn't make them up if you tried. And they're serious; that is, they all have a Message.

Alcohol inspired some of the songs: "I'd Rather Have a Bottle in Front of Me Than a Frontal Lobotomy." Nice turn of phrase, actually. Or, "She's Actin' Single—I'm Drinkin' Doubles." And there's a candid admission in the tune "If Whiskey Were a Woman I'd Be Married For Sure." And a morbid finale is offered in the song, "The Pint of No Return."

More important than drinking was the sad and recurring spectacle of love gone bad, love unrequited, or love gleefully terminated. There's something delightfully blunt about "Divorce Me C.O.D.," or "Thank God and Greyhound She's Gone." And can you picture "I Got Tears in My Ears From Lying on My Back Crying on My Pillow Over You," or the plaintive request, "Walk Out Backwards Slowly So I'll Think You're Walking In." There's an embarrassed admission in one tune, "Thanks to the Cathouse I'm in the Doghouse With You."

And when passion begins to wither on the vine, "Your Negligee Has Turned to Flannel Nightgowns" says it all.

Some of the most provocative and colorful song subjects were inspired by the God-fearing beliefs of country folk. Celebrating the importance of Christ can adopt a sports theme: "Drop Kick Me Jesus Through the Goal Posts of Life." There's a media reference, "Would Jesus Wear a Rolex on His Television Show?" A rodeo theme offers, "I've Been Roped and Throwed by Jesus in the Holy Ghost Corral." And the touchingly sentimental "She Was Only Seven When She Was Called to Heaven…(that Little Kid Sister of Mine)."

120

A couple of titles seem to raise questions of gender identity, although hard to prove without knowing the lyrics: "She Feels Like a New Man Tonight," and the puzzler, "My Uncle Used to Love Me But She Died."

Quaint, charming, honest, and maybe inelegant words. But sometimes linguistically complex and fresh, providing a glimpse into the mindset of Grand Ole Opry hopefuls. And according to language maven William Safire, the words of Country songs are a "unique American art form."

They are, but I don't think the maudlin message of "I Got Tears in My Ears…" will ever rival the fierce loyalty of "Stand By Your Man."

Cruising in My Kayak

I started dreaming of settling my bulk into the cockpit of a sleek, seventeen-foot fiberglass craft called a Kayak (or a "qujaq" in Eskimo talk) and with measured rhythmic and harmonious strokes of the double-bladed paddle, gracefully gliding across the water.

Like a skilled Alaskan Inuit or Aleut native, I'd fit snugly into the womb-like cockpit and imagine myself pointing the sturdy, maneuverable little boat into the frigid waters of the Bering Strait in hunt for a sea mammal, a mess of fish, or maybe even a caribou for my family's supper. (With my body occupying virtually every inch of kayak space, my dream gets fuzzy about where I'd store a sea mammal or a caribou. Do Inuits attach a floating trailer to their kayaks?)

The dream was inspired by a recent visit from Chicago friends who wanted to learn something "Lowcountry" before they moved down here. Like kayaking, for instance, though I'm not sure that's listed among Lowcountry delights like shrimping, crabbing, oyster or pig roasts. They quickly found a local business that rented the craft, provided instruction on operating the boat without running into sandbars or toppling over and drowning, and offered a four-hour package—two for instruction, two for open water challenge.

Their first kayak encounter was a bust. Tides about to shift—so no open water adventure today. Besides, given the amount of wobbling, tipping, bumping and almost capsizing our friends enjoyed during the two-hour instruction period in a practice pond, they realized that postponing a two-hour paddle on the high seas—or low Creek—was a brilliant idea. (They got a rain check.)

Hearing the comical and daring details of Chicago Braves vs. Lowcountry Kayaks inspired me to fantasize a bit on the kinds of pleasure I'd get trying to become a kayaker. My only exposure to water sports, I confess, has been limited to occasional holidays aboard cruise ships, each about the size of Peoria, IL, and with a passenger capacity that seemed like the population of Lower Manhattan. The solitary experience of being stuffed into the cockpit of a one-person, fifteen-foot kayak would surely be a refreshing contrast to the delightfully overindulgent hedonism of a 150,000-ton Empress of the Seas.

Maybe, though, there might be a compromise between the joys of kayaking and cruising. Maybe it might be possible to slightly modify a kayak to incorporate a few features and pleasures of a "Love Boat."

For instance, a small lifeboat lashed to each side of my craft would provide real peace of mind in case of a sudden storm, a leaky boat, a few curious sharks. The lifeboats would be supplied, of course, with food, water, first aid supplies, emergency flares, short wave radio, and a hook-up to the Global Positioning Satellite to help me locate in which snaky channel of the ACE Basin I've gotten totally lost.

If possible, I'd hope my kayak could be designed to accommodate an intimate lounge. Nothing ornate, of course. Maybe a half dozen tables, a small dance floor and, if the kayak's hatches can be widened just a bit, a piano bar. Not a grand piano, mind you. We don't want to sink. A baby grand would do. Or even one of those compact digital jobbies that Yamaha has been marketing lately. The company, I'm sure, manufactures waterproof models.

Most importantly, my kayak would accommodate (a small redesign of the hull may be needed) a casino. Nothing elaborate, of course: one craps table, three blackjack tables, and ten slot machines. After exhausting periods of paddling, a few visits to the casino could relieve muscle strain and, with a bit of luck, supply the Jackpot cash needed to pay for my unique kayak.

Other embellishments, of course, are possible. But we must be selective. I don't, after all, want the family kayak to turn into Cunard's QE II or Holland America's Maasdam.

On second thought…maybe I do.

Reluctantly, I may need to recognize the impracticality of my modified kayak. It won't work. Residents living along Battery Creek would surely raise hell over the raucous jangling of slot machines or the boozy bellowing of old pop tunes around the piano bar in the lounge—the Kayak Kozy Korner.

Besides, there isn't a caribou within a thousand miles.

Talent Search

The need for fresh blood in the pop singer business is insatiable. Especially of the nymphet variety.

The national supply of pubescent and post-pubescent superstar girl singers must be constantly replenished to satisfy the fickle loyalties of the teenybopper CD and concert ticket buyer.

The Brittanys, LeAnns, Brandys, Mariahs or Indias who currently illuminate the pop cosmos may fall from grace—or, worse, from the charts. Replacements must be found and manufactured quickly into slick and sensuous teen pop divas.

To avert a drought of singers, music agents, promoters, and record producers may be forced to run the following ad in the show biz bible, *Variety*.

FEMALE SINGERS/ENTERTAINERS WANTED

Convulsive Records, an American subsidiary of Young Water Lily Industries of Taipei, Formosa, is seeking female vocalists.

JOB REQUIREMENTS

Age Range: 13 to 16.

Personality: Sunday school, girl-next-door innocence with an undercurrent of rampant sensuality that threatens to erupt at any moment.

Versatility: Comfortable in all musical genres—pop, rock, jazz, hip-hop, blues, crossover, folk, country, ethnic, gospel—with the knack of making them all sound alike.

Musical Ability: Candidate must have a vocal range and total command of three to four notes, and sing them reasonably on pitch. She must also demonstrate the ability to count to four, with more or less even spacing. Lyrics must be delivered with total incomprehensibility, creating an aura of out-of-control ecstasy.

Physical traits: The navel area—from two inches above the belly-button to two inches below—must be free of all scars, blemishes, warts or hair. Fans consider an exposed midriff an infallible indicator of real musical talent.

Body Art: Tattoos are a plus for the candidate. Acceptable locations are the shoulders, waist, belly, thigh and calf—body parts that enhance performances by gyrating, quivering, shuddering, twitching.

Abstract designs are preferred, but patriotic symbols or tribute to one's mother are encouraged.

Bodily Movements: Torso, hips and legs must be limber and agile, capable of executing discreetly seductive dance steps that convey the rapture the singer feels while performing any of the three to four notes. During gyrations, if the tattoo images seem to "come to life," so much the better.

Related Actions: Candidates will be expected to demonstrate their affectionate rapport with a live audience. An aptitude for spontaneous waving, winking, and blowing kisses will be a key factor in the decision process. Candidates will be asked to wave, wink, and blow kisses at the judging panel.

Media Interview: Candidates will be required to participate in a practice interview to evaluate their skills in handling TV appearances on the Leno, Letterman or 700 Club shows. Subjects like family life (growing up with no indoor plumbing), sex life (too young to make a commitment), support of worthy causes ("I'd never wear *real* goatskin") and dedication to a Drug-Free America are OK topics.

Parental Approval: If invited to audition, applicant must provide a notarized letter of approval from her parents that certifies their willingness to surrender their daughter to the tender ministrations of music producers, promoters, agents, stage managers, sound techies, band members and hair dressers. Also, to allow her to cross state lines without violating the Mann Act.

Application Submission: Send 8x10 glossy photo, audition tape and Birth Certificate to Selection Panel, Convulsive Records, 100 Rising Star Blvd., Nashville, TN where the auditions will be held. Transportation costs to Nashville are the responsibility of the applicant.

Winning candidates will receive a one-week performance contract at the Yee-Haw Barbecue and Bar Roadhouse in Stillwell, Oklahoma.

Town Heroes

In the remote and rugged mountains of the Sierra Juarez in the Mexican State of Oaxaca, there's a native culture called Mixe ("MEE-hey").

The residents of the small Mixe village have an abiding passion for music. Indeed, they have a saying that seems remarkably sophisticated for rural folk: "A town without a band is a town without life." It is inconceivable to them not to have a band; it is their prized possession.

The Mixe band is a volunteer group of amateur musicians—farmers, artisans, and shopkeepers, we'd guess—who will never be invited to perform at an elegant Mexico City concert hall. But they don't care. Their mission is to instill their hometown with *muy* identity and pride. They see themselves, in fact, as part of a network of small, local bands that operate in virtually every town in Oaxaca State, in virtually every small town in Mexico.

The network of native instrumental groups is what binds communities together.

And when communities, for whatever real or imagined grievance, start feuding, they don't send lawyers or politicians to settle disputes. Who trusts lawyers or politicians?

They send their bands to serenade each other.

The Mixe, in fact, operate their own music conservatory to help strengthen hometown musical skills. But there's a hitch. Lessons are free, but graduates pay with different coin; if they move away, they must agree to return occasionally and perform in their hometown, and to visit villages that need a musical pep talk. There's only one nagging problem: there's almost never enough money to buy or repair musical instruments. So when, say, a trumpet player retires or dies, the horn is turned over to a youngster eager for the privilege of joining the band.

We had the pleasure of being in Oaxaca City on a Christmas Eve a few years ago. It was celebration time, parade time.

Marching around the *zocalo* (city square) at dusk were the usual assortment of local dignitaries and church officials, smiling and waving. They were greeted with a smattering of polite applause.

126

Following them were lavishly decorated floats bearing statues of beloved saints. The last float, surely the highlight of the procession, carried a radiant young schoolgirl, seated on a throne, dressed in a flowing white gown—the Virgin Mary.

All the floats drew respectable applause from the crowd lining the parade route. But it was the band that stirred the greatest enthusiasm.

Stepping proudly down the street were maybe a druggist, a realtor, baker, laborer, dentist—all lifelong residents of Oaxaca City—enthusiastically playing familiar tunes, both merry and martial. The crowd called out the names of several players, who responded to the greeting by dipping their instruments, or waving a drumstick.

They wore uniforms, of course, that had a quaintly improvised look—part soldier, part matador, part mariachi. No one cared if the jackets didn't exactly match or didn't always fit. It didn't hurt their playing. In the eyes, ears and hearts of the locals, this was a band of heroes. The musicians were, after all, friends, neighbors, relatives, looking and sounding grand, smart and proud. There was a genuine outpouring of affection and respect for the band as it marched by. We were so deeply moved by the reaction, we found ourselves cheering along with the locals.

As the band moved on and the sound of clarinets and trumpets faded, we wondered where in the U.S. could we have the same experience? Where could we go to watch, enjoy and clap our hands to a stirring march tune played by a local dentist (snare drum), a tax assessor (sousaphone), a city councilman (flute), insurance broker (trombone) or deputy sheriff (tuba)?

In New Orleans, maybe. But only to honor ones who died.

The Mixe town band tradition plays to honor and enrich ones who live.

Apology in the Dark

My wife must have some Slavic blood in her.

Russian playwright Anton Chekhov was a master of creating characters who would carry on passionate monologues with inanimate objects. At some point in most of his plays, a character might glare at a piece of furniture—a desk, say—and launch a one-way conversation. "Desk, how can you just sit there without feeling, without tears, while my beloved cherry orchard is dying under a woodsman's axe! Do you care? Do you suffer? Weep, foolish old desk!"

The desk would, of course, remain totally unmoved by the mournful plea, and just sit there without so much as flipping a drawer handle.

At a local movie house recently, my wife revealed a Slavic instinct that would have delighted Anton.

She talked to a wall.

We arrived a bit late, the theater lights already darkened. The only illumination came from the faint glow of a coming attraction on the screen. The glow was less than faint, the preview showing a murky and scary scene of a homicide cop finding a dead body in an alley dark enough to rival the Black Hole of Calcutta. Hardly suitable for finding seats.

We couldn't see them, much less which were occupied, which empty. But she bravely penetrated the dark chamber while I held open the theater door to let in a little corridor light—an act I was certain would provoke threats from the patrons sitting near the back. But a few snarls were better than my wife stumbling or falling. Within a few seconds she had virtually disappeared down the left aisle. I'd catch fleeting glimpses of what had to be her extended arm probing the darkness for seats along the left side of the movie house, a location where, typically, seats are arranged in pairs.

Now she vanished completely. A few more seconds passed. (Luckily, the patrons in the back rows were so absorbed in the horrific and bloody action on the screen, no one yelled at me about the open door.) My eyes were now better adapted to the gloom, and I spotted her further down the aisle.

Then her voice—whispered, distant, apologetic.

"Excuse me...are these seats taken?"

128

A few more steps, then "Oops…Sorry!"

Her seating predicament did not go unnoticed. A gentleman rose from his aisle seat in the center section and moved toward my wife. He gently touched her shoulder with admirable Lowcountry politeness and said, "Excuse me, ma'am. That's the wall. The seats are over here."

This particular movie house, it seems, didn't have pairs of seats along the left side. If my wife looked mortified, no one saw it.

The screen now brightened—daytime, a chase down a city street—allowing her to spot a couple of seats near the center. She beckoned. I let the door swing shut and joined her.

If next year's Spoleto Festival features an all-Chekhov tribute, I'm certain she'll be invited to audition for a role.

If she can apologize to a wall, she can certainly chew out a desk.

Part Five
Business

Dear Fellow Shareholders

I'm a modest investor in the whimsical, weird, volatile and aggravating phenomenon known as the stock market. When I'm not convulsed with the urge to wring necks, slit throats or cut out the hearts of corporate CEOs, day traders, or pontificating market gurus, I read the Annual Reports of the companies that are using my money to create global empires.

The Reports are impressive: 40-50 pages long, 80-100 lb. coated stock, five-color separations, stunning photographs of smiling executives (usually in dark suits), dedicated employees (also smiling), and ecstatic consumers. Mostly an exercise in self-adoration, the Report always opens with The Message from the chief honcho.

The Message usually contains such stock phrases as "I am pleased with the accomplishments of 2002..." or "We use strategic assets and intellectual capital as we build..." or "I am very excited about the opportunities ahead of us..." or "We are entering a dramatic new stage...."

Whoever writes The Message for the CEO apparently draws upon a lexicon of puffery and spin that makes him or her worth every nickel of the $150,000 annual salary. What I really wish for is a straight-talk, unadorned, blunt, this-is-the-honest-to-God truthful statement of what happened in the last fiscal year. A Message, for instance, that might read:

> Dear Fellow Shareholders:
> I'm writing this myself. Yeah, that's right. I'm hunting and pecking on my Toshiba laptop—a gift from my orthodontist brother-in-law who worked on me for six months and I still have an overbite—because the guy in my PR department handed me eight pages of drivel that would make even the dumbest stockholder gag. Stuff like: "a fruitful year" and "we look forward with radiant optimism to the future." Would anybody believe that? I don't.
>
> Actually, our merger with Waste Regeneration, LLC—basically a pig farm in Bulgaria—was a disaster. Those stupid porkers just didn't produce enough poop to regenerate. So how was I supposed to know

that? The closest I ever get to a pig is when my wife lets me have three slices of bacon once a week. I inherited, you see, my father's cholesterol problem. My doctor is making such a bundle on me, he bought property in Puerto Vallarta. Even *I* don't own property in Puerto Vallarta.

OK, so we had to shut down operations in nine plants this fiscal year. Our dedicated employees went on strike. Something about wages and benefits. I was really confused. Our pay scale now, my CFO tells me, is already up to the level of Wendy's, and our employees never smell like frying hamburgers. Ye Gads, what else do they want?

Which brings me to this flap about my compensation. You think 2.3 million a year is a lot? As CEOs go, I work cheap. You know what Mike Eisner makes over at Disney? Or Bill Gates, that skinny guy at Microsoft? Hey, with four kids, two still in college, I need every square inch of my 6,200 square foot house. You won't believe what it costs to keep those orchids alive in the greenhouse!

And I do a lot of company business at our summer place on Nantucket, where I keep my Boston Whaler. I'm a good fisherman, so we keep food costs down. And I haven't gotten a bonus in three months!

OK, so our P/E was flabby, and our share price dropped to a nauseating low. Not to worry. A lot more investors will gobble it up at $8.00 than at last week's price of $92.00. What a deal! The ladies of the Sunset Years Investment Club of Dubuque will go bananas. And who's to blame? Those moronic Bulgarian pigs.

The annual meeting is in three weeks. Don't come. All we're going to do is approve Scrooge and Marley as our Auditors (ha-ha, a joke!), and to see if we can get Jimmy Carter, Norman Schwarzkopf, or Ringo Starr to join the Board. (OK, I was a Beatles nut.)

That's all for now. So I'll end by saying that we look forward with radiant optimism to the future.

And a bonus.

My doctor says there's a nice piece of oceanfront property....

134

Paradise for Sale

The numbers are staggering.

They boggle the brain, congeal the blood, and curl the toes.

If a recent report is accurate, most of the virgin land in southern Beaufort County will become wall-to-wall houses, apartments, condos, and businesses. It evokes an image that is spookily reminiscent of Levittown.

Let's play a numbers game: on the drawing board are 30,000 acres, destined to accommodate some 18,300 homes and commercial enterprises. Add another 8,600 homes when the build-out of Sun City is complete. That's 26,900 homes. Add the D.R. Horton projects (another 696 houses), and we're up to 27,596 homes. Not by tomorrow, of course. But within a decade....

The game goes on. Assuming an average of 3.5 people per house, that's 96,586 new County residents. Each home unit will have, nominally, a two-car garage (or a triple, if you've got a boat or golf cart), or 55,192 vehicles contributing to the rapidly congesting County roadways. (One can almost sniff another road-widening Bond issue somewhere down the pike.) Each home will have at least three bathrooms, or a total of 82,788 toilets which, if flushed simultaneously, could lower the Savannah River by three feet.

I don't know the formula for calculating how many new schools (teacher shortage be damned, eh?), new Fire and Police stations, EMS services, sewage treatment plants, or traffic signals will be needed. And the tons of tarvia for new roads that will surely confound the earth's ability to absorb water.

There's no way of knowing how many trees will be cut down—a live oak, Oops! sorry—and torn up by their roots, compromising the stability of the soil.

And no way of knowing how the current residents of the 30,000 acres—deer, birds, squirrels, alligators, raccoons, quail, duck *et al.*—feel about being threatened, displaced or killed.

With natural disasters becoming more frequent, and with the housing market growing while the land is shrinking, James Lee Witt, the head of FEMA, reminded us that expanded residential and commercial construction "impedes natural protection against flooding—paving our open spaces and cutting down trees."

But expanses of choice, undeveloped land—to tax-hungry bureaucrats, bankers, investors, architects, home building suppliers, contractors, furniture and rug merchants—are irresistible, and epitomize the old saw: Nature abhors a vacuum. Empty space: fill it. Capitalize on it. Rub hands. Salivate.

Not too long ago, there was a Mayor of Portland, Oregon, who almost threatened to station police at all roads entering his city. Visitors were OK. Anyone who wanted to move or develop there would be turned away. No more "growth," thank you. Population is big enough, and we don't want to degrade the character, appearance, natural resources or lifestyle of the city. Thank you for your interest, said the Mayor, but turn around. Go build your 5,000 home units in Tallahassee.

I wonder if he'd like to run for public office in Bluffton.

1-800

What mortal with even a smidgen of dignity and sanity has not fought the impulse to scream, maim, or kill while entrapped by the automated answering devices so popular among American businesses? "Have a problem? Simply call our toll-free 800 number and one of our trained service representatives will be happy to assist you." Right. And the Kremlin is in downtown Detroit.

It takes grit, determination, and the legendary patience of Job to survive the disembodied voice that offers the "menu" of options for your selection. "Press 1 if you…Press 2 if you…" Usually, of course, the option you want—like why the new toaster is making belching noises, or why my kid has been trapped for two weeks in your Jungle Gym—is not offered.

It's reached the point where using a toll-free number requires a lot of careful planning: a day off from work would help; food and water within easy reach of the phone; close proximity to the bathroom (a cordless phone is a plus); and, if it's available, Valium.

It's the waiting. And worse than the waiting is the music they pipe into the line, presumably to divert and pacify you. Perhaps, if you had a choice of music—a Bach Partita, maybe—it wouldn't be so bad. But you don't, and the stress grows.

Automated phone service has taken hold and spread like a California brush fire. It's become easy to fantasize, therefore, the following encounter (after a wait of one hour, forty-three minutes):

"Hello. Thank you for calling the Diggum, Depe and Quigley Funeral Home." (Celestial organ music begins.) "How may we serve you? If the loved one is already deceased, press 1. If you anticipate that the loved one's departure is imminent, press 2. If no one has yet passed on but you wish information, press 3."

(I press 1)

"Thank you. If the remains of the loved one are at home, press 1. If the remains are in a local hospital, press 2. If the remains are out-of-state or within the Western Alliance Nations, press 3. If the remains are those of a family pet—dog, cat, hamster, goldfish or snake—press 4 and hang up."

137

(I press 2)

"Thank you. If you are planning a casket funeral for the loved one, press 1. If you are planning a cremation for the loved one, press 2. If you are planning a cremation and you wish to receive the ashes, press 3".

(I press 3)

"Thank you. If you wish us to arrange for floral tributes, press 1. Appropriate vocal and instrumental renditions, press 2. Engage the services of professionally trained mourners, press 3. Provide clergy, suitable to your religious convictions, press 4. Prepare the eulogy, suitable for both newspaper publication and framing, press 5. Arrange for Perpetual Care of the gravesite, press 6. If you wish…"

By now, the choked-back tears are draining into my throat, my hands are trembling, a migraine is beginning to loom behind my left eyeball, my knees are jelly. I hang up.

A fantasy, of course. No self-respecting funeral homes would abandon their carefully nurtured tradition of intensely personal attention. Unless, of course, they are seduced by the technological wizardry of the "products" offered by AT&T, Sprint or MCI—the siren song of the obedient, tireless, accurate, loyal and non-salaried computer chip. No enterprise can long resist the competitive edge and operational efficiency promised by eliminating real people.

But they can rebel. At the Duke Power headquarters up in Charlotte a few years ago, a former CEO issued a stern and shocking memorandum to his staff: subjecting customers to the impersonal, mechanical, automated voice is gone. Out. Kaput. No more. His action made *The New York Times*.

If the rebellion fails to spread, there is only one recourse for frustrated consumers. Fight back.

"Hello. Thank you for calling the Golden residence." (Music seeps into the line: "The Ride of the Valkyrie.") "We can respond to your call more fully, swiftly and graciously if you will please select one of the following options:

"If you are calling to request a contribution to save African Termites, Mongeese, Pygmy Elephants, or any other species of mammal or reptile, please press 1 now.

138

"If you are calling to seek support to free Tibet, feed North Koreans, house Rwanda refugees, or any other specie of human bipeds, please press 2 now.

"If you are calling to offer unbelievable deals on flood insurance, long-distance phone service, vinyl home siding, dirt fill, tree-pruning, or lake-side vacation bungalows in Nigeria, please press 4 now.

"Thank you. If you have pressed 1, 2, 3 or 4, both you and your phone will self-destruct in fifteen seconds."

Windfall

B less you, George W.
Your devotion to tax reduction has an almost ecclesiastical tang. It has a Crusader-like power and piety. It has a monomaniacal fervor that confounds the opposition and sends John Q. Public into spasms of joy.

Didn't we see those three typical tax-paying families, barely able to control their joyous spasms, arrayed behind you like stage props as you announced your tax-whacking plan?

After hearing your proposal to divvy up that $1.6 trillion surplus, I raced to my pocket calculator to figure what boon, windfall, deluge of cash I can expect to shower on me. I refused to be deterred by my total lack of knowledge about tax tables, tax brackets or tax credits. Recklessly, I punched in a few numbers, expecting to conjure up a vision of the unexpected wealth that would send wife and me to Tahiti, the Swiss Alps, or maybe to a Lexus showroom.

My calculator was either defective or malicious. It seemed to snicker as it produced an absurd dollar figure. Well, maybe a dab of oleo had stuck to my finger at lunch, making it slip on the calculator buttons. I punched numbers again. Same figures. Cheap, rotten little device! Then a third time. Curses! Same result.

My tax saving came out to a magnanimous $32.64.

What kind of passionate conservatism is *that*?

Taxes for a family of four were supposed to be reduced by $1600—"a year's worth of utilities in California" sayeth George W. We're a family of two. Why isn't my reduction at least $800.00? (Well, OK…we'll settle for a round-trip to Omaha or a down payment on a Chevy Cavalier.)

$32.64.

Being a practical fellow, however, I forced myself to ponder how I could maximize the largesse of $32.64.

How about buying one share of stock in Disney? (No. When I deduct my broker's commission, it would completely exhaust my manna from George.) Well, maybe two bottles of Concha Y Toro Chardonnay from Chile. (Naw. Wine gives me heartburn.) The $32.64 would buy me fourteen boxes of Drake's Devil Dogs. (Forget it. The added weight, expanded waistline and higher cholesterol would raise my doctor's blood pressure.)

Or I could try to make peace with our cranky pet by buying 65 cans of elegant Sheba cat food. (Nope. She'd complain even if we fed her ground filet mignon.)

Suddenly, a solution appeared.

I will donate the $32.64 to any organization dedicated to protecting the musk ox and the caribou from the depredations of oil driller rigs in any virgin territory of Alaska.

I'm *sure* our President, and his Interior Secretary, will be deeply gratified by this gesture of support and thanks.

Wal-Mart on the Potomac

Documents have been filed. A constitution drafted. Congress has been alerted. Within a year, Wal-Mart will seek admission to the Union as the fifty-first state.

It makes sense. Crowned by experts as the greatest retailer in postwar America, its employees probably constitute a population base larger than Idaho and Alaska. The acreage amassed to accommodate Wal-Mart Superstores (at 292,000 square feet a pop, plus vast parking lots—which, when empty, strongly resemble the Steppes of Eastern Siberia) is at least the size of Connecticut. Its annual revenue easily matches the GNP of Switzerland, Liechtenstein, and the Principality of Monaco—enough cash, in fact, to buy the Commonwealth of Massachusetts, including Martha's Vineyard and Nantucket.

A State motto, with a classy classical tang, has been proposed: *Non sibi sed cunctis*—"Not for one, but for many;" a State bird (Yellow-Bellied Sapsucker), a State flower (Venus Fly Trap), and a State flag (emblazoned with the sunny, smiling face of the Wal-Mart price-dropper) are under review by the Acquisition and Expansion Committee of the Wal-Mart Board.

A Commonwealth of Wal-Mart would set a standard of technological sophistication unrivaled by any other state; the company has a computer system that processes 8.4 million updates every minute—a data base second only to the U.S. Government. Microsoft, and other high-tech industries, would flock there.

The Commonwealth would also enjoy a strong international flavor: Wal-Mart has properties, thus far, in Canada, England, Germany, Korea, Mexico, and Puerto Rico.

Can Moscow and Beijing be far behind?

On second thought—given its financial muscle, the huge populations it serves, its exotic technology, its innovative marketing techniques, its management prowess, and its sensitivity to foreign relations—Wal-Mart should probably not aspire to become the fifty-first state. There's a much simpler solution: it should buy the District of Columbia—and run the country.

The White House, Capitol Building, and the assortment of other bulky Federal properties could move to Salina, Kansas—a nice, logical and *central* location. Salina would be awash in tourist dollars, a prospect certain to delight Bob Dole.

Besides, D.C. is not a state anyway. And it would be easier on tax-payers if we *didn't* have to cough up the megabucks to celebrate the admission of a new state.

Wal-Mart on the Potomac. A new era. A new destiny for the nation. Prices dropping on Band-Aids, khaki pants, aircraft carriers, postage stamps, and missile launchers. Reduced prices on political treaties that even Iraq couldn't resist. Senior citizens at Reagan National greeting arrivals with a warm smile and a shopping cart.

Don't you love it?

I do. I'm a Wal-Mart shareholder.

Made in...Where?

From her scarf to her sneakers, my wife is a walking global market. I didn't realize how global she was until I was persuaded (shanghaied, more precisely) to accompany her on a quick shopping excursion to buy a pair of slacks—"you know…something simple, loose, comfortable." I agreed, expecting as a reward an equally quick excursion to a nearby Baskin and Robbins immediately following her transaction.

After some 30 minutes, she was still in the exploratory stage of shopping; eyeballing the stock, decoding the display and rack system, memorizing the location of "Reduced" signs. I was about to make the usual meek protest, when I happened to glance at a label on a pink sports jacket.

"Made in the Sultanate of Oman."

Mexico, China, Japan I can deal with—but the Sultanate of Oman? I mentally surfed the planet to locate Oman. North Africa? The Middle East? An island off Borneo? Sultanates are—or used to be—ruled by Sultans, very rich nabobs with scimitars clenched in their teeth, and harem ladies flouncing enticingly to seductive flutes and drums. Has the Sultan abolished dancing girls and hookahs in favor of Economic Development? Is there a big unemployment crisis in Oman? Could the U.S. be throwing contracts at the Sultan for pink ladies' jackets to deter him from making the Bomb or buying Cuban cigars?

Such idle speculation was, at least, keeping me distracted from my wife's meticulous inspection of what seemed like 2,000 pairs of slacks offered by the store and the imminent round-trips to the dressing room.

Where else, I wondered, do these clothing articles come from?

I turned over a label on a silky blouse. "Made in Macedonia." Wasn't that once part of Greece or Yugoslavia, or both? I didn't suppose the tag would say "Macedonia" unless there *was* a Macedonia somewhere—complete with flag, national anthem, ethnic food delicacies, and lots of unpronounceable names.

I began to find such cultural and geographic ruminations pleasant. So I abandoned all hope of getting the "let's go" signal from wife, and continued my global journey. Where would it take me?

144

To the Orient, of course. To defuse political frictions, a "Made in Taiwan" skirt was at least twenty-four inches from a "Made in China" skirt. Deterring the People's Republic of China skirt from invading the Nationalist skirt were several sturdy items "Made in Macao," acting, I assume, as a peacekeeper. Remaining aloof, a few racks away, were unruffled blouses "Made in Korea." A pair of red shorts "Made in Hong Kong" (a favorite stitchery of Liz Claiborne) was nearby, clearly anticipating its takeover by Communist China.

Ralph Lauren, it seems, has a particular regard for Singapore sewing machines.

On to the Middle East—to Egypt, Dubai, and the United Arab Emirates, producing items for the U.S. like unto the sands of the desert. My command of global geography is shaky at best: I thought Dubai was a *part* of the United Arab Emirates. Maybe that was last week. (Some 30 feet away, like crossing the Negev, were "Made in Israel" suits. The separation was clearly an expression of political discomfort with its Arab neighbors.)

Turning, I got an indulgent "just be patient a bit longer, dear" smile from the wife as she pushed the wire cart bearing a mound of slacks to the trying-on room. At least Phineas Fogg had his Passepartout for company. I had to continue circling the globe alone, fingering little silken labels while sales clerks and customers raised one or both eyebrows at my perverse behavior.

My travels took me to Southeast Asia, where products for the American consumer are "Made in Indonesia" and "…in Malaysia," where the hum of sewing machines is woven into the background music for exotic temple dancers.

Drifting accidentally over into the men's section—where an America First chauvinism should prevail—I found a team windbreaker jacket emblazoned with "UNC Tarheels." Made in Thailand.

Glancing to my right, I wasn't sure whether my wife, still pushing a cart, was going to or coming from the dressing room. I concluded she was in a holding pattern until a changing room opened up.

Moving on, I discovered dresses "Made in Turkey," some cute socks "Made in Bulgaria," and knit polo shirts from the C.I.S.; that is, "Made in Russia." The Cold War is definitely over.

Finally, a signal from my wife—a jerk of the head toward the exit. The abruptness of the motion said: "there's nothing here!" Evidently, not one of the 2,000 slacks was the right size, color, style, fabric, texture, flair, *panache*, or sale price to suit her. Which is OK. Some of the unspent money will end up at Baskin and Robbins.

But the revelation about the global sources of ladies' wear (I fondled the labels of some twenty-seven nations and remote islands) made me wonder. Like whatever happened to those passionate marketing efforts by American unions (I.L.G.W.U., notably) to persuade Americans to "buy U.S.?" The promos don't seem to be on TV anymore. Or did they become futile and hollow in the face of American corporations scouring the planet, ravenous for cheap labor?

I'd buy a shirt that said "Made in the U.S.A." (Van Heusen hires locals in Honduras and Indonesia.)

If I could find one.

For Sale

Corporations love it. They salivate over the chance to pump millions of sponsorship dollars into competitive sports events and to savor the sweet benefits that exposure, prestige, influence, and product sales will produce.

Like the Kilroy graffiti of WW II, corporate products and logos are endemic: on NBA scoreboards; on the walls of hockey rinks, baseball parks and tennis courts; on the programs of golf tournaments; and from radiator to tail pipe, plastering the skin of racing cars, turning them into hurtling billboards.

And with prizes approaching cosmic proportions—the bait to lure the superstars—the deep pockcts of Budweiser, Coca-Cola, MCI, and Winston are a blessing.

The roster of sponsors could, in fact, come right out of the Fortune 500 list of Goliath companies. (Fortune 500, eh? A natural for an auto race sponsor at the Charlotte Motor Speedway.)

Tennis has its du Maurier Canadian Open, the Toshiba Classic, and the Acura Classic. Golf has its Sprint International, MCI Classic, Mercedes Championship and Buick Open. Even fishing has its Bass Masters Classic.

But for a sheer, unequivocal cascade of sponsors, it's auto racing: Auto Stores National, Winston Cup, Busch Grand National, Miller 200, Coca-Cola 500.

And there's lots of co-op buy-ins by Citgo, Ford, Goodyear, Dupont, and even Goody's Headache Powders—a must, one would think, after 500 miles of nerve-shattering and bone-jarring RPMs.

The stage is set. The monied characters are out there, in place, eager to find new forms of combat, new markets, fresh opportunities to capture the eye, ear and wallet of the American public. A floodgate of creative sponsor tie-ins is waiting to burst open.

A sampling of a few such choice and logical opportunities comes easily to mind.

The Mister Kleen Baptist Boycott Regional: a competition to determine which sect will eradicate Disney from the Christian planet.

The One-A-Day Beach Bully Open: a prize for the largest amount of sand kicked in the face of 100-lb.weaklings by 250-lb. cretins.

147

The Ben and Jerry Bovine Insemination Championship: 50,000 waffle cones for the producer of cream that contains catastrophic levels of cholesterol.

The Di-Gel Hot Dog Eating Nationals: finalists must qualify by cramming 100 wieners down their gullets in five minutes. Whoever is alive at the end wins.

Kellogg's Snap-Crackle-Pop Wrestling Classic: orthopedists and radiologists at ringside to certify whose tibia cracked first.

The Chun King Governmental Influence International: a lifetime supply of soy sauce for correctly tracing the flow of Oriental soft money into political war chests.

The mightiest of all competitions, the one that utterly polarizes the entire nation, that penetrates every household, that provokes the most feverish debate at bars, barbershops and barbecues, and that guarantees the emergence of the most visible, powerful and familiar figure—the President of the United States—is ripe for sponsorship.

The campaign for the U.S. Presidency, given its numbing duration and astronomical costs, is a juicy plum ready to be plucked by one or more enterprising corporations.

Many of these corporations already invest millions to underwrite the campaign for any number of motives—altruistic or otherwise. Let's be fair, open, candid. Quid pro quo. We're in a sponsorship-ridden culture, in which just about everything is "brought to you by…" (Hey, if former Senator and Presidential Candidate Bob Dole—a solemn icon of probity and personal dignity—agreed to pitch credit cards on national TV commercials, protocols have changed: the cow's jumped over the moon.)

Can't you just see it? January, 1999. President-Elect Al Gore—or is it Dan Quayle?—appears for his swearing-in, ceremonially dressed in his Jeff Gordon coveralls, decorated like a Christmas tree with vivid corporate logo patches.

Over his left breast, GM; over right breast, GE; over his heart, Bank of America; just above his navel, Archer Daniels; on his left shoulder, Boeing; on his right, AT&T; on his left forearm, Microsoft; on the right forearm, Exxon. On his back, a kaleidoscope of patches declaring the support of Prudential, Pepsi, IBM, Texas Instrument, Hershey, and Dr. Scholl's Foot Powder.

148

As the final touch: stitched to his blue cap as a testament to his patriotic fervor, American Express.

The apotheosis of the Advertising Age has been reached. The happy *menage a trois* of Commerce, Culture and Politics is now consummated.

Well, almost. There's a big-time Marketing VP casting a hungry eye toward some hot competitive events in the Middle East....

Where's the Hoisin Sauce?

I t's priced right. It's popular. It appeals to all ages and to all religious, national and ethnic groups. And you can go back for seconds, or thirds, loading up your plate with a small mountain of selections from the steam table.

Where are we?

At a Chinese buffet restaurant, of course—surely one of the most widespread and familiar eating establishments in the U.S. No, let's modify that—in the world, from Oaxaca, Mexico; to Kassel, Germany; to Sydney, Australia—and many points in between.

The appeal of the steam table offerings is really simple. Drive your payloader up to the food bar and load your plate (or take-out box) with fried rice, pork, chicken, beef, broccoli, egg drop soup, wontons, noodles and the inevitable defrosted and warmed-up egg rolls.

My wife and I enjoy it often, gleefully filling bowls and piling up plates, and coming away happily stuffed. And contrary to popular myth, we are *not* hungry an hour later.

But for the record—and in the interest of historical and culinary authenticity—most Chinese buffet-style restaurants don't offer Chinese food. They serve Americanized Chinese food—a menu that has, for the most part, abandoned the ritual, history, celebration, and culinary traditions that have for centuries made Chinese cuisine among the best and most honored in the universe. (Better than French, some argue, though it raises a few Gallic hackles among the folks at Cordon Bleu.)

OK, so what's special about *real* Chinese food?

Joyce Chen, a restaurant owner and chef in Boston, will declare: absolutely and unquestionably fresh ingredients. Ms. Chen shops every morning in local markets. When the produce, fish or meat has been selected, only then is the menu prepared for that day.

At an authentic Chinese dinner, each entrée will be served individually—one at a time. Each food, the Chinese recognize, offers a unique texture, flavor, taste, appearance and aroma. You don't ruin it by mushing two or three dishes together.

A real Chinese dish will appear at the table looking beautiful, making the diner want to devour it with his eyes and causing the mouth to water in anticipation.

150

In a pavilion near the summer palace of the Dowager Empress in Beijing, our American delegation (of which I was a member) was served lunch. The first course was hot and cold appetizers (meat and vegetables). When the dishes were removed, chicken with bamboo appeared. The plates were cleared and a whole roast duck was served. Dishes cleared. Then a whole fish, followed by a lobster dish, then a turtle dish, then soup. Buns stuffed with bean paste and soft dumplings wound up the "light" lunch.

The Chinese would never pile one food on top of another. It would dishonor the food and show contempt for the chef.

To the Chinese, food is a celebration of life, offering both a spiritual (all things must be in balance) and a cultural dimension. There are dishes named for great historical figures, dishes to honor famous poets or scholars, dishes to show respect to ancestors, or to celebrate a holiday. (I suppose a hot dog salutes Mr. Frankfurter—but it's not exactly the same.)

And there are unique and sometimes strange ingredients that never excite the palate in buffet places: pickled ginger, cassia bark (like cinnamon), Szechwan Peppercorns, Star Anise and Sea Cucumber. (With all respect to Chinese culinary choices, this last item is revolting.)

We'll continue to patronize local Chinese buffet establishments. It's a good deal, it's tasty, it's plentiful.

Besides, we can't afford the airfare to Beijing.

Getting Labeled

I haven't written my name and return address on a piece of mail for at least the past five years. I may have forgotten how.

Thanks to the financial hungers and marketing gimmicks of some twenty-six national organizations, I am regularly supplied—nay, swamped, deluged, inundated—with what appears to be the fund-raising strategy *du jour*: sheets of peel-off, self-stick labels imprinted with my name and address.

Among the agencies sheltering me from the ordeal of scribbling my name and address are the Diabetes Association, Defenders of Wildlife, Doris Day Animal League, Center for Marine Conservation, and the National Committee to Preserve Social Security and Medicare. And with all the announced tax refunds on the way, maybe the CIA and FBI will be obliged to send labels and solicit donations.

By actual count—and my wife witnessed me carefully toting up my current cache of labels, so I'm not cheating—a desk cubicle contains 2,637 labels. Some printed with my name; some with my wife's; some Mr. & Mrs.

They come in virtually every color of the rainbow, in a dozen different type fonts (medieval to computer); some bold and manly in design, others delicate and feminine.

But, ah…the illustrations, the art work that embellishes the label are meant to appeal to whatever your mood, whatever the occasion. Feeling hungry? Feast on images of gingerbread cookies, candy canes, mushrooms or strawberries. In a patriotic mood? Peel off an American Flag or an American Eagle. Crazy about wildlife? The labels offer a cornucopia of air, sea, and land creatures: dolphins, turtles, wolves, bears, foxes, butterflies, and geese. Stoking up some Christmas spirit? Use the labels featuring Santa, Christmas trees and baubles, snowmen and snowflakes. A little nostalgia for New England? Use the labels with autumn leaves or the one with corn stalks. And if you're in a cuddly mood, there are cute kittens, perky puppies, and rollicking rabbits.

It's really a little sad, though, having 2,637 crisply printed and gaily decorated address labels, patiently waiting for the chance to brighten some important correspondence—my fan letter to Julia Roberts, maybe, or a note of deep thanks to the Chairman of the Lottery Commission for the nice check.

But that's fantasy stuff. My labels are reduced to strictly utilitarian uses—like on the pre-printed envelopes supplied by utility, telephone and sewage providers. And that's only three labels a month. At that rate, my supply will last for 73 years—or until I'm approximately 140.

The labels, alas, are a dying breed. My computer will print my return name and address on an envelope faster than I can peel off a turtle, snowflake, or pussycat. And with a delicate keystroke, my Microsoft infested Gateway will print labels in any of two dozen typefaces and in color.

The *coup de grace* for the freebie labels is, of course, E-mail. And an even bigger blow to the label-making industry is the mental and literary laziness that's made Americans listless and indifferent letter-writers—an occupation that was once a high and cherished art. (We'd have known nothing about our Colonial history without the letters of Washington, Jefferson, Madison and many others.)

I'm now down to 2, 636 labels. I used one on the envelope to dispatch this piece to the *Gazette* Editor.

It's a comfort to know that, in your lifetime, there's something you'll never run out of.

The Four Billion Dollar Snicker

Y ou can almost hear the muffled snicker and spot the skeptically raised eyebrow when you say it: "The availability of cultural resources contributes significantly to a community's 'quality of life.'" Yeah. Sure.

Or to produce an audible guffaw, try: "And this culture-generated quality of life can impact directly on the economic health and future of a community." Right. And the Tooth Fairy is my uncle.

Some years ago, up in Malone, NY—that State's North Country—they weren't snickering or arching eyebrows. And it wasn't guffaws we heard; it was lamentations.

The North Country, back in the late '80s, was eager to be selected as the site for the construction by the U.S. Department of Energy of a $4.4 billion—yes, you read it correctly, $4.4 billion—superconducting super-collider (SSC) that would wither, crush, decimate and smash atoms back to the day they were born.

(Why we would subject helpless atoms to this denigrating treatment eludes my right-side brain.)

A 53-mile underground tunnel would be needed to house the high-tech donut, requiring 4,500 persons to build it, and some 2,500 home-buying, grocery-shopping, tax-paying folks to run it.

How about that for an economic impact on Malone's hardware store?

But the good folks in the North Country didn't make it. They didn't appear on the list of finalists for the behemoth project.

Where did they go wrong? Why did an area of the State that enjoys an abundance of very tangible assets—the right seismology, geology, state and local assistance—have to face the melancholy experience of witnessing a $4.4 billion opportunity (the Ultimate Plum, surely) be super-collided out of existence?

The intangibles. The Feds, with unexpected wisdom, wanted "quality of life" things also—employment opportunity for spouses of SSC workers, nearby universities for new learning experiences.

And in the words on the rejection slip, "proximity to cultural resources."

154

It's simplifying, certainly, but not unreasonable to suggest that for want of a ballet school, four billion bucks was blown. For want of a choral society, 4,500 construction jobs were vaporized. For want of an art gallery, the vision of 2,500 permanent jobs became dust.

It's exciting but nerve-numbing when one's articles of faith turn to fact; when a stunning validation of one's gospel is manifested in this magnitude.

But all we can do is commiserate with the good folks in the North Country. The SSC project would have been an incredible boost for the whole Upstate NY region.

But let the moral not be lost on civic and political leaders. It's really true—Culture Means Business.

Go snicker up your sleeve.

Toot—Groan

It sounds like a dying Banshee. Or a constipated cow. Or the cries of lost souls moaning in Hell.

It's not a steam whistle anymore. It's a mechanical horn that groans with a melancholy and piercing sound that announces: This train is moving. Beware! Stand Clear!

The Port of Port Royal, once the target of irate residents whose houses and vehicles were coated with a mysterious powder-like substance exuding from the Port, now supplies a new form of invasion—the strident cacophony of the diesel engine warning signal. When the horn blows, a front porch chat with neighbors is abruptly suspended. Hands cover ears. Hurling uncharitable epithets at the train is useless. They can't be heard. A cannon shot wouldn't be heard.

OK, so the old whistle is now a new horn. Progress, I suppose. Its mournful wail signifies the passing of yet another bit of nostalgia, of Americana.

The steam whistle, for some 150 years, meant that the ol' 519 was coming through, right on time. Set your clocks by it. Things were right when things were regular.

The steam whistle meant power—the superheated water in the boilers letting off a little steam while driving the rods that turned the wheels.

The steam whistle meant freedom, escape; of seeing farmlands and lakes and mountains. Or maybe getting to savor a little big city life in Atchison, Topeka or Santa Fe.

It meant the knitting together of a nation—the states all connected by endless ribbons of steel track.

And the steam whistle meant railroad legends embodied in folk song:

"He was comin' down the track doing 90 miles an hour,

When his whistle broke into a scream…."

In an altered form, the steam whistle meant the throaty notes of carnival calliopes; of a circus troupe marching down Main Street while the Bearded Lady threw kisses; the acrobats leaped, tumbled and rolled; the clowns performed clever capers.

156

And it meant enraptured kids straining along with the Little Engine That Could—chug, chug, puff, puff, "I think I can. I think I can." The funereal horn at the Port seems to be moaning, "I think I died. I think I died."

Vintage stuff. Nostalgia, maybe. Rapidly eroding memories of an early, expanding America.

Sorry, but a train signal that sounds like a wailing Banshee or a sick cow just doesn't make it.

Holding It Together

J ohan Vaaler, clever as he was, never made a dime—or a krone—from his momentous little creation in 1899.

A student of engineering and mathematics, the Aurskog, Norway native started bending and twisting a length of wire until it assumed the familiar double parallel form of what is now universally recognized and esteemed as the Paper Clip.

Unhappily for Johan, Norway had no patent laws in 1899, but Germany did. For some obscure reason, royalties never made it to Aurskog.

OK, so the humble paper clip has never been immortalized in poem or song. It will never rank with the piston engine, penicillin, or liposuction. It never broke a sound barrier, inspired a mechanical heart or cloned a sheep.

But try to imagine planet Earth without this miniature and versatile giant.

When you think of it, paper clips have wide and sometimes weird applications. Holding together a stack of papers is the very least of their achievement. Other uses have to include the paper clip as bookmark, as money clip, as staple remover; it will hold a hem that needs sewing or become a hanger for curtains, lights or pictures. It can pick locks, puncture balloons, or temporarily secure a bra strap. Not recommended and hazardous uses: cleaning out earwax or, with a cleverly manipulated rubber band, making a lethal missile.

The paper clip was even used as a gesture of defiance. During the WWII Nazi occupation, Norwegians were forbidden to wear a lapel that bore the initials of their King. Instead, they flaunted and taunted the Germans by replacing the pin with a paper clip—to the natives, a symbol of solidarity against the invaders.

In a world torn by sectarian strife, a paper clip doesn't give two figs for religion. It is utterly non-denominational, comfortable, and compliant in the hands of Muslim, Jew or Christian. It will, without malice, suspicion, or anger as readily hold together a stack of Bar Mitzvah instructions, a list of altar boy assignment sheets for next month's High Masses, or the six pages of the Holy Koran that a future Imam must study to prepare for a stern examination.

The paper clip, like a faithful and loving dog, is totally indifferent to rank or station in life. It will obediently hold sheet-to-sheet for a serial killer or a king; an elected official or a scam artist; a corporate CEO or accounting firm VP; a U.S. President or a pickle-slicer at the Stage Deli. A paper clip knows only its destiny: to hold documents securely together. The hand that uses it is totally irrelevant.

There is something to be learned from this lowly but eminently functional little object: stay loyal to what you were created to be.

The paper clip deserves, at the very least, an annual national holiday. Perhaps a 14-stanza tribute by a Poet Laureate, or captured in a 30-foot steel sculpture dominating the D.C. Mall. The issuance of a commemorative stamp by the U.S. Postal Service would be very nice; the composing and dedication of a symphonic poem maybe.

To involve young people, an essay competition open to every seventh grader in the world. The topic: "Imagine the Universe Without Paper Clips." The essay must be at least three pages long—held together, of course, by the subject of the piece.

It is time we honored this inventive, versatile, practical, unglamorous, inexpensive and global creation. Johan Vaaler's descendants deserve no less.

The appropriate measure of tribute to Rubber Bands, Post-Its, and Thumb Tacks will, in the fullness of time, be bestowed by a grateful nation.

10-10, Here I Come

My telephone bill makes fascinating reading.

Not because it has any literary merit, a deficiency shared with utility, water and cable TV bills. You won't find yourself at a cocktail party entertaining the company by reciting a merry quip or two courtesy of Sprint or ATT.

What's intriguing, and just a little alarming, is the stunning, and probably still growing, list of ancillary costs that fatten the bill, most of which defy comprehension.

Sure, I'm comfortable with and ready to pay a reasonable cost for calling a neighbor next door or a son in California.

But when confronted with a list of obscure and inexplicable add-on costs, whose origin and meaning are as remote as the Dead Sea Scrolls, I feel a heartburn rising in my gorge and a migraine stabbing at an eyeball.

My bill listed a total of fourteen additional expenses: four "Charges," four "Surcharges," three "Taxes," two "Funds," and one "Fee."

I added up the costs of "Emergency 911 surcharge," "Interstate access surcharge," "Federal universal service fund," "Number portability surcharge," "Telecommunications surcharge," "Franchise user charge," "SC Universal service fund" (two costs), "Universal connectivity charge," "Federal tax" (two costs), "State tax," "Municipal license fee," "Regional call charges," "Bill statement fee," and the vague "Other charges."

The total additional cost was the equivalent of 39% of my monthly bill.

I called an 800 number for an explanation of certain charges. The response was, of course, a disembodied, automated voice, offering a list of "options." My option was to hang up. I suspect that the explanation would have been as dense and unhelpful as the charges themselves.

Would sweet and loving Ma Bell have done this to me?

But being a charitable fellow, and knowing how needy mega-corporations can be, let me propose three more potential revenue streams that Sprint, ATT, MCI, 10-10, and other phone service providers are welcome to adopt and use.

MOLE DETERRANT SURCHARGE. Needed to underwrite costs of applying Moltox and rat poison to discourage moles from nibbling on underground cable. Also to cover medical bills incurred by company employees who accidentally confuse the chemicals with Pepto-Bismol.

BIRD DEFECATION DEFLECTION FUND. Pays for experimental devices and strategies to discourage avian droppings on working linemen, such as shrill noisemakers, bronze gongs, and Rohmer elephant guns.

EQUITABLE EXECUTIVE COMPENSATION ENHANCEMENT TAX. Revenues dedicated to improved salary/benefits/deferred income package for those executives who conceive and impose the most subtle, irritating, obscure, redundant, frustrating and burdensome extra charges on naïve and helpless customers.

If I can find a phone service out there that doesn't hammer me with a "Number Portability Surcharge" or a "Universal Connectivity Charge," I just might switch.

Tax Creativity

A cat and a dog as tax write-offs?

A pair of tax consultants from Little Rock thought so. And they're both in the slammer now—one for six-and-a-half years, the other (who ratted on the first) for one year.

Their crime? They advised clients to deduct a cat as "rodent control." They also persuaded the client to write off a German Shepherd as a "mobile security unit."

Innovative? Certainly. Creative? Almost. Punishable? Definitely.

The sentencing judge remarked, "Any person of average intelligence should have known there was something not right about this." Not an especially eloquent opinion, but accurate.

It's a little sad that this burst of imaginative expense reporting should be frowned upon. After all, who with most of his wits intact can fathom, interpret, and apply the new, revised, and monstrously expanded federal tax code? Can the writers of the code? Doubtful.

As a service, therefore, to other imprudently creative tax advisors, here are a few other opportunities to enjoy guest quarters in the Federal Prison System.

Applying the screwy logic of our incarcerated tax guys and praying that a tax return is reviewed by a pressured and overworked IRS auditor with vision rated at 110/95, an enterprising, daredevil tax consultant might consider as write-offs:

—A canary, including the cost of the cage, perch, cuttle bone, and a six-month supply of bird seed. Rationale: a defense against noxious and deadly fumes.

Like the warning to coal miners of old, if the bird gags and then drops lifelessly to the floor of the cage, a deadly miasma has invaded the house. Surely the IRS would not deny an American homeowner the right to protect his family and reduce the cost impact on HMOs, thus avoiding a Federal bailout.

—Garbage Compactor. Rationale: suitable landfill areas are dwindling rapidly. Compacted trash occupies less space, thus minimizing the threat to the environment. Protecting the environment is, at the very least, an act of patriotism. The IRS, in this era of international tension, would surely not abuse a patriot.

162

—Atari Computer Games. Rationale: the sharpened eye-hand coordination, the quickness of response and the hypnotic concentration will prepare a family's teen-agers for survival on America's highways and freeways. Heightened reaction time will reduce accidents, lessen the need for police patrols, control road rage, reduce taxes for law enforcement, eliminate traffic tie-ups, and save on precious fuel reserves—surely a commendable and deductible act of public service.

Any tax advisor is welcome to use these tax write-off strategies in the preparation of the 2002 Federal tax return.

But not mine.

Heartburn Heaven

W hen did a cure for acid reflux—heartburn, to us overindulging peasants—become a religious experience?

When Nexium—the "Purple Pill"—descended like a blitzkrieg on millions of TV screens.

We've known for a long time that there's always a sly, subliminal message in TV commercials. Makers of body, skin and hair potions aren't selling creams, oils or lotions. They're selling Eternal Youth.

Diet products are only incidentally related to the slendering of lumpy bodies. They're actually pitches for the Irresistible Sexuality that a lithe, shapely, and sensual figure will declare to the world.

Cures for arthritis, migraines, nasal congestion, and assorted allergies may or may not cure anything. But the promise of Freedom from Pain spawns big hopes and bigger dollars.

And what do the maddeningly redundant car commercials promise—sleekness, color, speed? Not really. It's Machismo—masculine virility and ego.

If a product is a cure for a medical malaise, it will usually conclude with a not-so-subtle suggestion: politely arm-twist your family MD into writing you a prescription for the pharmaceutical magic bullet that's advertised at least 116 times a day on network and cable channels at great expense to the pill producers.

But Nexium raises the sub-text message to spiritual heights. In the TV ad, hordes of people, like pilgrims driven by some Biblical imperative, defy cliffs, crevasses and craggy hills to reach relief from—fear, deceit, sin? No. From Acid Reflux.

To its credit, the commercial has the spectacular intensity of a C.B. DeMille production as the hordes ("a cast of thousands") fervently and joyously swarm to the top of the Mount to find a Holy Grail of blessed relief and salvation. And they are moved, at times, to give "testimony" to the power of the sacred pill.

It evokes—despite the digital manipulation of monster blocks of stone—the image of hordes of Indian faithful leaping into the sacred Ganges to be purified. Or the hordes of lemmings being driven impulsively and uncomprehendingly to the top of a cliff—and jumping over.

164

Glowing with rapture and mystical uplift, the Nexium pilgrims overflow with brotherly and sisterly love, offering their hands to help fellow heartburnites to struggle up the Mountain of Hope and Salvation. And as the ultimate epiphany, receive the Purple Pill and be forever free of the burning curse of Acid Reflux.

What a production! What a budget! What a lot of unemployed actors getting work!

The commercial is better than a re-run of "The Newlywed Game."

It activates my acid reflux.

I'll chew a Tums.

Selling to Survive

Mournfully watching its reserve account dwindle into oblivion, the Clark County School District (Las Vegas) was ready to take desperate measures to cope with the unhappy prospect of a $13.3 million shortfall.

One source of untapped revenue suggested by the District's Finance Officer was to sell ads on school buses.

Horrors! Exploiting vulnerable, innocent school kids by exposing them to the greedy machinations of Madison Avenue hucksters?

You bet. And very smart. Don't parents usually succumb to pressure from their kids to buy a toy, a game, a hip cap?

And it surely won't be long before other reputable, non-profit, public service agencies may discover the cogent and appropriate reasons to improve their bottom lines by selling something.

What agency, for instance, needs to replenish its coffers more rapidly than the U. S. Treasury—an organization struggling vainly to cope with looming deficits. Maybe with just a nod from the President, promotional signs might be hung discreetly around the necks of the historical, heroic figures in Statuary Hall, a site visited by millions of consumers annually.

George Washington, for example, could display the sign: "Sarah Lee—Our Cherry Tarts are Revolutionary." A small banner across Thomas Jefferson's chest would read: "Burpee Seed Company—We Grow Legendary Tomatoes." And on Ben Franklin: "Kinko Prints Almanacs."

Closer to home, our State Legislature, that tax-starved gang, would be prime targets for windfall fees from commercial ads. To improve its fiscal anemia, two 30-second commercials will alternately appear after each roll call vote on the TV screen built into the desks of all the Honorables. One spot will promote Milk of Magnesia; the other, No-Doz. The revenues from both will fatten State coffers while directly addressing two classic ordeals commonly suffered by elected officials: indigestion and persistent drowsiness.

And churches, of any denomination. Like any other competitive not-for-profit, it costs more these days to spread the good word and encourage purity and righteousness. The cash flow solution is simple:

before the service begins, a large TV screen will appear above the altar. The congregation will rise in silence to experience a 60-second video ad for Chock Full O' Nuts Coffee. The product is entirely appropriate to the setting. The product does, after all, promise "that heavenly flavor." And would the Metropolitan Opera House scoff at the generous income from Warner-Lambert's proposal to be the exclusive distributor of Hall's Mentho-Lyptus Cough Drops to opera audiences? Certainly not, given the skyrocketing salaries of sopranos and tenors who have been known to threaten decapitation of any audience member who coughs or even clears his throat.

The momentum has begun. I'm convinced there's an ad agency out there already casting an enterprising eye on a South Dakota mountainside. The colossal faces of four presidents…hmmm…wonder if we can sell that to…

Sign Mania

Once upon a time, a sign was simply a piece of information. A couple of centuries ago, it was a quaint, dignified, handcrafted object that hung on a bracket over a shop door. Need trousers? Head for the "Clothier." The stuff to load in your pipe? The "Tobacconist" was ready. Or a powder to rouse your wife from the "vapours?" Look to the "Apothecary" sign.

Nothing crass, glaring or hucksterish. Simply: Here's what we offer. Step in if you need us.

These humble graphics couldn't satisfy the ballooning entrepreneurial and competitive hunger of American business for very long. The rough wood of rural barns became a primitive billboard promoting products like Red Man Tobacco. The whimsical jingles of "Burma Shave" signs appeared, easing the tedium of driving on long country roads.

It was French engineer Georges Claude who changed the sign game forever. In 1902, he created the neon lamp. In 1910, the neon light—later dubbed "liquid fire"—revolutionized an industry.

Times Square was the first great legacy of Georges Claude. And he actually lived long enough to witness that cacophony of illuminated, dancing, pulsating images hurled at us from every side. A later generation of sign designers—armed with neon tubing, LED and fiber optics—began to create glowing messages with a visual stridency that cried: "Look at me! At ME!"

Monsieur Claude's second offspring is Vegas, where the darkness of night is forever banished. Vegas is a sensory overload of dazzling light designed to heighten the excitement of casino action, superstar performers, and monstrous jackpots. Vegas signs have become the ninth, or maybe even the eighth, Wonder of the World. It's amazing that the human retina can survive the visual orgy.

Advertising signs have become warriors, battling for the public eye, heart and purse. They're not about information any more. They're about persuasion, enticement, seduction. They're about out-flashing, out-glowing, out-tantalizing competitors in a market place that bombards the hapless consumers with a clutter of aggressive imagery.

168

Too aggressive, apparently, for the civic officials up in Myrtle Beach. Back in 1995, City Council gave billboard companies seven years to remove 111 signs that created "visual clutter and distraction." Now, seven years later, the companies argue that the City's action violates their First Amendment right to create visual pollution. And so, heigh-ho, off to court they go.

From the genteel, hand-crafted "Apothecary" sign (the type still in use, incidentally, in the charming downtown of Victoria, BC), to the Red Man ads on the sides of rural barns (an image now cherished by Americana buffs), to the whimsy of the roadside Burma Shave messages (still out there in remote corners of the U.S.), to the garishness of Times Square and Las Vegas, commercial signs have evolved explosively over the past century.

And still evolving—upward. Drive any Interstate, and at an Interchange over the next hill there's a forest. No, not trees. Signs. Towering some 80-100 feet like skinny fingers pointing at the heavens, enticing you to patronize Cracker Barrel, Denny's, Day's Inn, Burger King, Chevron, Exxon, Ramada, Shoney's. From a mile away you can spot them, looking like stripped trees, inviting you to Exit now for comfort, food, rest—while violating the natural environment.

To paraphrase a popular jingle: "I think that I shall never see, a signpost lovely as a tree. Indeed, until the signposts fall, I'll never see a tree at all."

Same Place – Different Memory

W hat a surprising and pleasant way to be stirred into a nostalgic mood.

I refer to the effect of the piece by my fellow *Gazette* "regular contributor"-in-arms, Scott Graber. In the Sunday, October 27 edition, he recorded with melancholy accuracy, his encounter with a struggling institution in Central New York—the languishing Hotel Syracuse.

Ah…the Hotel Syracuse. It was, for nearly a quarter century, my second home.

It was where I ate, drank, partied, conferred, sang lustily at the Tack Room piano bar, conducted all manner of business—cultural, political, financial and romantic.

Back in the late '60s, the Hotel had not yet fallen into the depressing traumas and sad prospects so ably reported by Scott. Yes, the parking was awful then, too. And the ominous stirrings of chain motel developers along Interstate 81 were just starting to unsettle Hotel management.

But it was still halcyon times. Syracuse City and Onondaga County were awash with dramatic ideas for new parks, a new Community College, strategies to clean up polluted Onondaga Lake and—the crowning project—a new government center that combined a sixteen-story County office building with a three-theatre performing arts complex.

My job, from 1966 to 1973, was to prove that the theatre complex was a viable, vital and critical element in making Syracuse a progressive and sophisticated town. And then, if it got built, to run it.

My base of operations: the Hotel Syracuse. It was neutral ground, centrally located, familiar and comfortable to all classes of residents.

It was here that we interviewed prospective consultants, architects and builders. Here that we'd ply with very dry martinis the Chief Editorial Writer for the major newspaper, urging him to take a strong stand in support of the Center. (Two days later his editorial appeared, threatening the Seven Plagues of Egypt on any County Legislator who voted against the project.)

It was here, on the back of napkins, that architects embellished, re-configured and modified theatre designs. (Need to get from front-

170

of-house to backstage without going outside. Syracuse weather, you know!) Here that corporate leaders were stroked, cajoled, promised almost anything (name a theatre, name a room) for a hefty contribution to an Endowment Fund.

And it was here on Opening Night (January 15, 1976) that the Hotel Syracuse hosted a glorious gala in the 10th Floor Ballroom for everyone—all 2,200—with an Opening Night ticket. Plus a supply of complimentary mini-suites for out-of-town family, friends, and media VIPs.

Perhaps the next time Scott chooses, or is obliged, to stay at the Hotel Syracuse—with its Main Lobby that always enjoyed a shadowed elegance—he might stroll the three blocks (turn R. from the Onondaga Street exit) to the Civic Center. Right at Columbus Circle.

Is it still there?

If it is, it's as much a tribute to the Hotel Syracuse as it is to its planners and users.

Part Six
This and That

A Genome Fantasy

O n June 15, 2067, the breathlessly awaited letter from the GSRL (Genetic Selection and Reproduction Laboratory) reached the home of Gerhard and Gertrude Klotznagel. It was a fairly thick letter, which delighted the Klotznagels because they knew it contained The Questionnaire. It was a document sent only to those couples approved by the PDM (Population Management Division, est. 2048) of the Department of Health and Human Services.

The Klotznagels were ecstatic. By a national lottery, they'd been chosen to have children in 2068, and the Questionnaire would allow them to create a precise profile of the desired offspring. The GSRL would take care of the rest—selecting, splicing and inserting the exact genetic code needed to realize the Klotznagel's dream child.

Indicative of how sophisticated genetic manipulation has become by 2067, here's a sampling of the decisions the Klotznagel's had to make.

The Freedom of Information Act supplied us with a copy of the Questionnaire:

1. Sex of Child: Male___ Female___ Hermaphroditic___
2. Number of Children Desired: 2___ 4___ 6___ 8___
   (Note: the chemical base of the genome occurs only in pairs.)
3. Hair Color: Black___ Brown___ Blond___ Vermilion___ Puce___
   Mauve___ Burnt Orange___
4. Eyes Color: Blue___ Grey___ Green___ Basalt___
   Aquamarine___ Lilac___
5. Facial Features: Hairy___ Hairless___ Thin Lips___ Full Lips___
   Roman Nose___ American Nose___ Narrow Nostrils___
   Flaring Nostrils___
6. Physical Stature: Short___ Medium___ Tall___ Sinewy___
   Slender___ Willowy___ Obese___ Gigantic___
7. Disposition: Cheerful___ Moody___ Shy___ Serene___
   Wimpy___ Fun-Loving___ Anti-Social___
8. Athletic Aptitude: Contact Sports___ Bowling___ Badminton___
   Weightlifting___ Jacks___ Rollerblading___ Craps Shooting___

9. Cultural Skills: Piano___ Guitar___ Harpsichord___ Graffiti___
   Sousaphone___ Video Poker___
10. Career Aptitude: Scientist___ Doctor___ Attorney___
    Librarian___ Croupier___ Auto Mechanic___ Cult Leader___
11. Handedness: Left___ Right___ Ambidextrous___
12. Life Span: 50 Years___ 75 Years___ 100 Years___ Eternal___
    (Note: if Eternal is chosen, the subject will require gene alteration
    and replacement every 50 years.)

Shortly after the form is completed and submitted to the GSRL, Mr. Klotznagel will appear at the Lab to supply a sperm sample—his only duty in the process— the Age of Genetic Enhancement making any other form of participation obsolete. The sperm will be genetically modified to produce the exact specifications the parents requested. The Mrs. will report a week later for *in vitro* fertilization.

Nine months later—despite the genomic triumph, it still takes nine months—a pair of hermaphroditic daughters are delivered, with mauve hair, lilac eyes, hairless faces, Roman noses, willowy stature, fun-loving dispositions, a knack for jacks, a talent for the Sousaphone, a flair for auto repair, ambidextrous, and who will live forever.

Fortunately, I won't be around to see the unique twins. I never did have a taste for hermaphrodites with mauve hair or lilac eyes. But if they could change the oil and clean the carburetor…well, that's another thing.

176

The Legend of Max and Morris

O K, so I'm a Damned Yankee. You know, the Northerner who comes to visit, gets instantly hooked on the place, and decides to stay.

I wish I really deserved the label of Yankee. It would be a source of real personal pride. But I don't.

No ancestor of mine was a Minuteman, crouched behind a boulder near that "rude bridge" at Concord, ready to put a musket ball into anything wearing a red coat. None of my forebears were among the rowdy gang of fake Mohawk Indians who dumped some 340 chests of perfectly good India tea into Boston Harbor. No great-great-great uncle affixed his signature to that treasonous document called the Declaration of Independence. And the only Mayflower my family ever loaded stuff on was a moving van.

But if by Yankee you mean a passion to control your own destiny, to be enslaved by no one ("Don't Tread on Me" warned an early Colonial flag), to speak your mind in an open forum, and to be ready—Lord help us all—to fight an oppressor, then maybe I do have a touch of Yankee blood.

Not the New England variety, of course. Not the Bunker's Hill (Breed's Hill to the historical purist), Boston, Lexington or Town Hall Meeting variety.

More like the Shepitovka variety—a railroad stop deep in the sugar beet farms in the Ukraine of late nineteenth century Czarist Russia. It was probably the kind of village warmly depicted in "Fiddler on the Roof." But a village not so warmly viewed by the marauding Cossack troops who, wielding sabers and lances, periodically roared through the village to pillage, steal, burn, and sometimes kill a few locals.

The Czar approved these "disciplinary visits." After all, the residents of Shepitovka were non-people; they were prohibited from owning property, from voting, from practicing their religion, from holding public office. Not, however, from paying taxes.

It was in Shepitovka that Uncle Max (the hothead) and Uncle Morris (the strategist), imbued with a Slavic version of the Yankee Spirit, decided that enough is enough, already! These filthy Cossack thieves

177

and killers were robbing them of their identity, of their human rights, of their homes, gardens, livestock.

They decided to act. To this day—now over a hundred years later—the mystery lingers. Where did Max and Morris get the guns? Borrowed, bought, stolen? They'd never owned a weapon. Never held, loaded or fired one.

But now they each had a rifle and six bullets apiece. They didn't dare practice with the weapons. With a total of only twelve bullets, why waste them on tree stumps? No—twelve bullets meant twelve dead Cossacks—and a powerful message to the Czar: don't tread on us!

The guns were well hidden, they thought, from the eyes of their father, the village Patriarch: the stern, long-bearded, black-frocked elder, scholar, bible interpreter and one-man village judge and jury.

The old man found the guns, of course; nearly stumbled over them in the cow stall, poorly concealed under straw.

Remaining uncharacteristically calm, he summoned Max and Morris at once. He instructed the boys to pick up the weapons and follow him. They crossed the farmyard to the well and stopped. His silence was terrifying to Max and Morris, knowing how easily Papa could invoke the wrath of God, threaten pestilence and fire, invite the Heavens to groan and explode.

He raised an arm, bent his wrist, and pointed a finger down the well—and waited. The boys—their almost-rebellion against a pitiless tyrant at an end—dropped the rifles and the bullets down the well.

After a few seconds, the splash was heard. The father said softly to his sons: "If we kill a Cossack, we become a Cossack."

I can't claim Sam Adams or Ben Franklin. Just Max and Morris.

And the Cossacks, it turns out, even wore red coats.

178

Training to do Nothing

I tried to prepare for it. Honestly, I really did.

As a former academic, I'm comfortable with organizing and executing research projects, tracking down relevant documents, conducting personal interviews—the whole panoply of scholarly mechanisms at my fingertips. I wanted to be ready for retirement, to conduct myself in a knowledgeable, dignified, healthy and productive manner. To become, vainly, the apotheosis of Senior Citizenry.

At 68, and in good physical condition, I should expect—what?—another ten or even twenty years of low-fat, low-salt, no-cholesterol, brisk-walking and serene-thinking life. A life of grandchild-spoiling, of volunteer good-deeding, of hobby-reviving existence. I've read the literature. I know what to do.

But odd behavioral phenomena have surfaced that were unreported in scholarly and self-help literature. Little things, to be sure, but they take on monumental proportions in the context of a life that has been suddenly unplugged from the tasks, disciplines, and exhilarations of a professional career.

A brief catalogue:

Time. It has become a vaporous, ambiguous phenomenon. No longer measured in neat packages—rising, work, dinner, recreation—time drifts between two elements: daytime (when it's light outside) and nighttime (when it's dark).

The urge to set the alarm clock, a half-century ritual, still occurs and must be forcibly resisted. My hand reaches, stops—what are you doing, dummy?

Another question has begun to recur: what day is today? (My dental appointment was Monday, and that was two days ago, so it must be....)

Chores. Once trivial and annoying—and with some cunning, avoidable—"honeydews" are now greeted with alacrity and gratitude. "Let me take the cans and bottles to the recycle bin, dear." "Empty the vacuum cleaner bag? Of course, hon." Motivated by husbandly compassion? Not really. More like motivated by a hunger for relevance. I've got to have *something* to do.

179

Marching to the front curb for the Monday morning trash pick-up has become, Lord help me, a cause for celebration.

Foot Enlargement. A phenomenon never mentioned in the literature. Except for working in the yard or going to the Piggly Wiggly for milk, shoes have become extraneous, a relic of pre-history, anachronistic. Padding about in my old and loving slippers (or is it called "shuffling?") or, better yet, in stockinged feet—am I rehearsing dotage?

Furthermore, having occupied a new house—with somewhat pricey taupe carpeting—the wearing of shoes is unrelentingly taboo. The upshot is predictable: my foot size will surely increase from a 10 double E to an 11 triple E. By my 70th year, I expect to be dubbed Yeti. Big Foot.

Sartorial Decay. The suits, sport jackets, and dress shirts hang in the walk-in closet like forlorn, unwanted orphans. If paternal, I should at least protect them in plastic bags as an expression of sympathy.

The same for the two pair of dress shoes that probably won't fit next year. And neckties—heavily culled because of my wife's abhorrence for the indelible food stains I've attracted—hang like wilted banners.

It doesn't matter, probably. In this casual southern town, only lawyers and doctors wear ties—sometimes. Is it time for a pickup by the Salvation Army? (I should save at least one tie for medical emergencies. A tourniquet, maybe.)

The wardrobe, you see, was my career attire, my regalia of responsibility and authority. Having been mustered out of service, the wardrobe still torments.

Guilt. The sensation of being a truant, an AWOL, still persists, nags like a shrewish conscience. It's three o'clock Tuesday: is the agenda prepared for the staff meeting? (Don't let me forget to commend Leslie for the successful Funfest.)

It's the fourth Thursday of the month: why aren't I calling the Board Chair to discuss reappointment of the Nominating Committee? Has my assistant, Mary, issued the memo on staff parking policy revisions? I look at my wristwatch and—momentarily, irrationally—panic. I'm supposed to be at…

It will pass. Indeed, it's beginning to subside already, like the blessed passing of a migraine. But the guilt lingers. I'm supposed to be administering, directing, *leading*. And I'm not. Then I look down at my stockinged feet, and that's reality.

Going Native. An aberration, certainly. But suddenly bereft of both social and professional imperatives, a three- or four-day growth of whiskers has become inconsequential. For whom, or for what, do I need to shave?

A sport shirt is slightly stained by pasta sauce. The checkout girl at Winn Dixie doesn't even look up. And when we go out to dinner, and I forget to change out of my battered and grimy gardening shoes, the hostess, discreetly, never comments on the whiskers, sauce stain or dirty shoes.

My wife is, of course, mortified by my beach-bum appearance, and has begun to issue ultimata: "Change your shirt, fella" "Not in those shoes, guy." And naturally I'll comply, once my subconscious rebellion subsides.

Office Toys. I was surrounded by them: a fax, a behemoth copier, networked computers, a paper cutter with a blade that could serve as a guillotine. I had a huge stapler that could, I swear, penetrate a Manhattan phone book, and a supply closet—a cornucopia of pads, pens, paper clips, manila folders, sheet protectors—which, like the proverbial rabbit, seems to endlessly reproduce itself.

I loved them all. Not that I used them all, but they were there—reassuring, reliable, poised to deliver instant gratification. An administrative security blanket.

Not re-creatable in retirement. But then, why even necessary in retirement? Because, like a deep-sea diver ready to re-surface, if I don't decompress slowly, I'll suffer management bends—an acute and maybe terminal reaction to the absence of mechanical and electronic things that were part of the mix of my professional breath.

Thus, a computer desk (assemble-it-yourself) was purchased three months before retirement; a desktop printer and copier were acquired shortly after retirement—both of which produce documents at a molasses velocity. But what's the rush, eh?

No FAX yet, but a three-hole punch, a stapler, a Rolodex, a stack of post-it note pads and—glory be!—an electric pencil sharpener. I've neglected to mention my nine-year-old computer which is, at the very least, a collectible, if not an antique.

Yes, a modest assortment of office paraphernalia. But it's a comfort. It'll get me through.

And finally...

Priorities. There are none. Nature may have softened its attitude toward vacuums; they seem, at the moment, to be tolerated. The planning urgency and discipline normally experienced when, for example, I'm scheduled to confront the Finance Committee of the County Commission to plead for a higher budget allocation, dissolve into a tepid puddle when replaced by a casual excursion to some local discount outlet stores in search of bath towels. Or laying in a supply of Pop Tarts in preparation for a visit from grandsons.

Priorities—the infrastructure of management responsibilities—have become, at least temporarily, soft and ambiguous. The blood-rushing, nerve-tingling challenge of organizing battle plans has evaporated. Discount stores and Pop Tarts are not yet truly satisfying replacements.

And yet...

Enough rationality still prevails, however, to suggest that these unanticipated behavioral flukes are temporary, transient quirks. They're a manifestation of loss, a kind of bereavement period that occurs with the passing of a loved one—the career. I expect to recover from the period of mourning—weasel out of chores, wear clean shoes, put on a suit occasionally, shave more often, and recognize the high priority of Pop Tarts. Retirement will become my new career.

Ah, but...

Terra Firma

N ow here's a challenge—the Mother of all Challenges—that should intrigue South Carolina's cadre of noble, far-sighted evacuation planners: a wall of water, anywhere from 25- to 100-feet high, roaring onto America's East Coast. Not Japan, or Okinawa or Borneo, mind you, but the Carolinas, Virginia, Delaware, D.C.

Some geologists and geophysicists have discovered a crack in the floor of the Atlantic Ocean—the kind of wicked, gaping trench that can produce weird tidal behavior, creating conditions that can spawn a monster wave. A Tsunami.

This prospect is, according to the solemn scientists, not a matter of "maybe" or "if." It's a matter of *when*.

Disquieting, even shocking news. As they'd holler in the early Westerns, "Head for the hills!"

The experts have just discovered a crack in the Atlantic Ocean floor? Heck, I knew that would happen 52 years ago.

To satisfy the undergraduate science requirement at Tufts University, I enrolled in Geology 101—a perfect course for a math-challenged Freshman. The professor was a great bear of a man, at least six foot eight, with bushy eyebrows, and hands as big as elephant ears. He didn't deliver perfunctory lectures; he bombarded us with passionate sermons on the awesome, terrifying and unstable nature of planet earth. Nobody, absolutely nobody, slept in his class.

He knew it first hand, having explored the nooks, crannies and crevices of the globe; chipped away at the igneous, sedimentary, and metamorphic rock; prowled around the batholiths, monoliths, and erratic boulders; scoured the planet for evidence left by the implacably moving glaciers; measured the violent upheavals of the earth's crust that formed mountains. He'd felt the tremors of the tectonic plates at the earth's sub-crust, grinding relentlessly against each other, producing the shock waves that sometimes scored a ten on the Richter Scale, collapsing whole cities.

A real pro was Professor Robert Leslie Nichols. He'd been there, done that.

He set the theme of Geology 101 on the first day of class. He walked; no, he strode; no, he stormed to the blackboard and scrawled, in two-foot high letters, the words: TERRA FIRMA. He stared at the phrase for a few seconds, stepped back, turned to the class and roared HAH! To the bewildered freshmen, he announced with the solemnity of a royal decree, *"Terra is not Firma! It is a great lie! It is a delusion! The planet is alive and changing even as you sit here!"*

It was an ominous beginning. My fellow classmates nervously checked the floor and ceiling, certain the roof was ready to fall in or the floor to tear open.

Well, we all survived that semester, and for many years to follow. We absorbed his teaching and ended the term with a wary respect for the fragility and vulnerability of our planet.

An oceanic trench discovered along the Eastern seaboard? Of course. Why not? Any Geology 101 student knows that. "The planet is alive and changing…."

What we never learned, however, was the answer to one very basic question: if a tidal wave struck, would there be enough Firma Terra to get out of its way?

We never asked him that question. By the end of the semester, we knew his answer.

Goodbye, Old Friend

Sanity and survival finally won out.

I quit smoking. Not an easy decision, given that my bond with the pernicious weed goes back about six decades.

Few relationships in my life were more intimate, more persistent, more comforting, than between me and a pack of cigarettes. Crisis, confusion, anger, melancholy were bearable with a lit butt. Joy and rapture were magnified ten-fold when the match ignited the end of a smoke.

And is a glass of fine Scotch or an icy Corona truly satisfying unless accompanied by a Benson & Hedges 100's Deluxe Ultra Light? Thinking, writing, cocktailing—all were enhanced, fueled, and intensified by burning tobacco.

Cigarettes were a good friend.

OK, so there were compelling incentives to quit. Like breathing. Breathing is a very useful habit—unless, of course, you wish heart, lungs and assorted other internal organs to keep you alive at a level slightly lower than a fruit fly.

But to my great surprise, it's not the hot, searing assault on the throat, trachea and bronchi that I miss. It's not the volumes of yellow-gray glop that needed to be expelled with a regularity and quantity too ghastly to be described in a family newspaper like *The Gazette*. (Restaurant diners at a table near ours would often be seen whispering to their waiters, and then being reseated in some remote corner of the establishment. I rarely saw the hostile glance of waiters through the impenetrable smoke screen my beloved Benson & Hedges would produce.)

No, none of the above do I miss. What really saddens me is having to give up the game of challenging and outwitting the abundant smoke Nazis—that fierce, pious and pompous crew that would go to any extreme to prevent me from exercising my constitutional right to destroy my lungs and gradually suffocate.

Thwarting these butt bigots was a source of real delight. A challenge, a game. I'd arrive at an unfamiliar residence for a visit or a party—and immediately start the sniffing and the eyeballing. Any trace of stale cigarette smoke still lingering in the air, on the curtains, on the breath of the hostess? (The breath test can be tricky to execute discreetly; some hostesses get uneasy as your nose zeroes in on their mouths.)

Then the scan job. Eyes dart around the foyer, living room, den in search of burn scars on the furniture, or any object that even remotely resembles an ashtray.

This requires a special grasp of the history, style, value of glass or ceramic artifacts. The side table bears an octagonal object that looks, from a distance, like an ashtray. On closer inspection, it's—damn!—a piece of Murano crystal valued at some $2,000.00.

Failing any smoker conveniences inside the house, I now search for exit doors—to a porch, a garage, a breezeway. Where are they located? Can they be accessed easily? Unlocked? Sneak over and test the knob? Don't want to slip out for a quick puff and get locked out. Tacky, very tacky. The search has the quality of casing a joint before a heist.

But I do get outside, having found a door off a rear screened porch with no lock. Outside, I'd smoke blissfully, concealed behind a tall holly bush. (Smokers need to know a lot about the concealing and camouflaging characteristics of a variety of plants. Clemson Extension can, I'm sure, supply useful pamphlets on the subject.) I've also enjoyed a smoke behind a compost pile, knowing that most dinner guests don't explore compost during the evening's festivities.

Now that I've successfully confounded that anti-smoking homeowner, my final challenge is to dispose of the dead cigarette butt. Widely recommended is to always carry a small tin box as a portable ashtray; or an empty beer can or bottle is usually handy at parties; or the soil around a large potted plant is suitable in a pinch. Or simply field strip the dead butt (a skill supplied by the U.S. Army), find the guest john, and flush away the remains.

Then pop a tic tac in your mouth.

The subterfuges worked for years. Worked too well. The only one I subterfuged was me.

But we had some great times together, my friend and I.

The Imperfect Storm

There's nothing like the prospect of drowning in the North Sea to sharpen the senses, develop an appetite, and make a bottle of Scotch look like the Holy Grail.

As we strolled the deck of the newly renovated QE2, two large picture windows suddenly imploded, scattering shards of glass in every direction—an event not promised in the seductive cruise brochure. We knew that something ominous was happening. No staff, no crew were visible to warn passengers to forsake the deck chairs and get inside. So my wife and I did the warning.

In the early spring of 1987, we were aboard the QE2 for a New York to Southampton crossing. The ship, recently out of dry dock, showed signs of an incomplete refurbishing. Rolls of carpeting still awaited installation; metal pails were scattered around corridors to catch the leaks; debris of unknown origin floated on the indoor pool; the hot water tap in the cabin produced no hot water; and the cold water had a vague odor of diesel fuel.

The ship, one could guess, was not altogether ready to go back into service. But the bean-counters at Cunard evidently felt that a few leaks and a dab of diesel in the tap water should not impede revenues.

By ten that night, the ship was beginning to roll and lurch, causing passengers to lean against walls, against each other, grab handrails, clutch their drinks, their chairs. Objects began to slide off tables and crash to the floor. No announcements were made, either to warn or comfort.

We retreated to our cabin, bumping into bulkheads, staggering like drunks who weren't sure where to place their feet. And just in time. A bottle of good Scotch was within a hairsbreadth of sliding off the nightstand between the beds.

By eleven, the ship was beginning some serious heaving and listing. When a small TV receiver in the corner of the room tore loose from its moorings and flew across the room, we began reflecting on our mortality. (Ironically, the night before the storm I'd hit a slot machine for $1,000. How cruel, I thought. I could be heading for the bottom of the North Atlantic with ten crisp $100 bills in my wallet. Lord, just let me live long enough to spend them!)

187

It wasn't the loss of the money that alarmed my wife. It was the small curtain at the window. As the ship listed, the curtain hung almost straight out, at about a 45-degree angle from the wall. And stayed there. We clutched at our beds wondering if the ship would right itself. I thought about the instructions we got during the obligatory lifeboat drill. We figured that with all the pitching and rolling, with all the heaving up and slamming down, the last place we'd want to be was in a lifeboat. If we could find it. If the crew—most of whom, we later learned, were below being sick—could find it.

But the worst of all was the melancholy groaning of the ship's steel plates, which sounded like lost souls in Hell. Does the popping and cracking noise mean the plates will buckle?

I staggered to breakfast the next morning, the ship still rolling, wrenching, pitching. About twenty souls made it to the dining room, three of whom almost immediately toppled over backward in their chairs. Dishes, cups, salt shakers, coffee pots would rattle, tremble, then slide to the floor.

The storm, with a magnitude of ten on the Beaufort Scale—a scale that only goes up to ten—lasted nearly eighteen hours.

Two dozen people were injured. The next-door cabin mysteriously became icy cold, forcing the occupants to wrap themselves in coats, sweaters and blankets. A dozen glass-top tables were destroyed. A grand piano, flimsily attached only to the carpet, was demolished.

At about two o'clock the next afternoon, the churning, thrashing and groaning had stopped. The weary voice of the Captain finally came through the intercom: "...the worst storm I've experienced in seventeen years..."

There was a polite tap on our door. It was out room stewardess, a pretty young Londoner, who asked, "A bit hungry, are you?" We allowed as, yes we were, the recent terror having stirred our appetites. She nodded and left, returning in about a half-hour with a stack of sandwiches on a large tray.

She joined us for what we surely thought was a meal we'd never see. The miraculously rescued bottle of Scotch was opened, and for the next two hours we gobbled and drank, grateful that the villainous North Sea had spared us.

We arrived in Southampton a day late.

But we *arrived.*

188

Walter Mitty Lives

Every one of the 2,700 seats in the concert hall is filled by eight o'clock.

I enter from down right and stride briskly and confidently to the podium. The applause that greets me is friendly, but not ecstatic. But wait until they hear my interpretation of Beethoven's Ninth!

Mounting the podium, I wait patiently, benignly, until the coughing, throat-clearing, program rustling and chatter cease. The utter silence is my cue. I square my shoulders. Benevolently, but sternly, my eyes sweep across the 110 musicians of the Vienna Philharmonic and the 150-voice chorus standing on risers behind the orchestra.

Musicians and singers stiffen in anticipation, their eyes focused intently and adoringly on me. I don't need a score; I don't use a baton—my hands alone will shape and evoke all the subtle dynamics, tempi, shadings.

I raise my arms. Bows snap into position over the strings, fingers lightly touch the trumpet valves, mallets are clutched firmly by the tympanist.

My arms descend. Celestial sounds now fill the room...

No...it's my wife telling me that dinner is ready, and would I please get some paper napkins from the storage closet.

After dinner, coffee on the porch. But it's not the porch. It's the boudoir of Madame Tosca—and I'm the lecherous and sinister bass-baritone Scarpia. I'm lusting after the beautiful opera singer who has been scorning me in favor of a shabby artist—who I, as police chief, plan to imprison and torture. I'll have her tonight, by heaven, or I'll....

Oh, how I love to sing bad-guy roles—every note full of sneer, despotism and villainy. The personification of evil. No gray zones here—all slurp and slather, all bully and beastly. A less polite audience would boo and hiss, but not the polite season ticket-holders here at the Metropolitan Opera. But privately—oh, how they hate me and wait impatiently for Tosca to thrust a blade into my heart.

The moment comes. My lust is now blindly out of control. I make my move; she makes hers—with a dagger. How beautifully I die! I stagger backward in pain and astonishment. I writhe and stumble, reaching for the table to hold me. It doesn't, and crashes to the floor. I

189

drop on one knee and look beseechingly at my killer. In rage and triumph she shrieks, "Morte! Morte!" (Die—Die!) I drop to the other knee, clutching at the knife, fall on my back and try to rise again. I emit one final and very melodic howl: "Arggh!!" And die. The death bit will surely be worth a second or third solo bow at the curtain call...

The call I hear, however, is from my wife: "West Wing is coming on now, dear." Damn! I'm always interrupted at the curtain call. But, oh, how the *Times* critic will rave.

When you surrender fantasy, you surrender life. Fantasy is the fertilizer that nourishes the heart, the brain, the spirit. It makes the pulse quicken, contracts the muscles, tingles the skin. The dream of the last-minute rescue, an eleventh-hour cure, the winning lottery number, the wild acclaim helps us to survive reality. Besides, it hurts no one.

In bed now, and half-asleep, I realize we're touching down at the Oslo airport—and there's the limo bearing the Chairman of the Nobel Prize selection committee who smiles and waves at me as I start down the stairs....

Delectable Learning

In the classroom, kids learn to read, write, learn to say "How's your mother?" in Spanish, dissect a frog, watch chemicals hiss and bubble, discover what makes a triangle isosceles, and why Shays rebellion was a bust. Excellent.

In the cafeteria, they're offered pizza, barbecued ribs, hot dogs, corn dogs, steak biscuit, plus assorted veggies and desserts. The menu, no doubt, has been sanctioned by school dietitians as not only healthful, but also popular with the students. Very good.

But the gap between classroom and cafeteria is vast. In the former, students are loaded up with fact and formula; in the latter, they're loaded up with carbs, proteins, and sugar.

But what if we could close the gap? What if eating could become as powerful an educational tool as, say, an American History lesson plan?

What if the School Board was ready to adopt a deliciously innovative teaching strategy: Eat to Learn?

Really want to understand a foreign culture, or the customs and resources of Colonial America? Eat their food. It could be a savory method of heightening the gustatory appetite of students, help to make them discriminating and sophisticated arbiters of uncommon cuisines, and provide a very tasty way of learning the history, agriculture, lifestyle and family traditions of foreign lands, and our own as well.

Herewith, therefore, is a proposed educationally succulent one-week menu that the food service staff can easily whip together, one that will tantalize both the taste buds and the brains of students.

Monday: China (1.2 billion healthy people can't be wrong)
Appetizer: Egg and Watercress Dip
Main Course: Steamed *Chiao-Tzu* (a nice change from spaghetti)
Dessert: Sweet Rice Dumplings (eaten to honor poets)
Beverage: Green Tea (cures almost everything, the Chinese say)

Tuesday: Armenia (one of the first countries to adopt Christianity)
Appetizer: *Yalanchi* (stuffed grape leaves)
Main Course: *Madzoonov Mees* (roast lamb with yogurt)

191

Dessert: *Pakhlava Tertanoosh* (layered pastry with walnut filling)
Beverage: *Jajukh* (chilled yogurt, cucumbers, mint leaves, clove)

Wednesday: Greece (poetry, architecture, music, philosophy!)
Appetizer: *Skembe Avgolamona* (tripe soup with egg-lemon sauce)
Main Course: *Souvlaki* (broiled lamb in grilled pita bread)
Side Dish: *Tahini* (sesame seed paste)
Dessert: *Halvah* (cake)
Beverage: A glass of *ouzo* (but not taken on school property)

Thursday: Italy (DaVinci, Dante, Machiavelli, Sophia Loren)
Appetizer: *Cappelle di Funghi Ripiene* (stuffed mushrooms)
Main Course: *Calamari Fritti* (deep-fried squid, a Roman favorite)
Dessert: *Cannoli Siciliana* (beloved sweet climax to an Italian meal)
Beverage: *Chianti Classico* (grape juice will have to do)

Friday: Early American (the melting pot of world cultures)
Appetizer: *Schnitz und Knepp* (Pennsylvania Dutch—a soup/ham/apple/stew dumpling)
Main Course: Geoduck Steak (Northwest Territory—neck of gigantic clam, tenderized, seasoned, pan-fried)
Dessert: Pickled Peaches (an Old South Sunday dinner tradition)
Beverage: Sarsaparilla (medicinal, some say)

Well, it's a start. Subsequent weeks can feature delicacies from Kashmir, Oman, Myanmar, Kazakhstan, Liechtenstein, Thailand or Zimbabwe. The possibilities are deliciously endless.

In just a week's time—what a global culinary adventure! And think of the tie-ins with classes in history, social studies, languages! Think of the new bravado of kids who dared to try Fried Squid—and liked it. And think of the kitchen staff—tired of grilling hot dogs and scrambling eggs—now effervescing with joy over their new-found culinary boldness—and who will soon demand that they be sent to the Cordon Bleu in Paris for a month's training.

And what if the students don't like the unusual cafeteria cuisine? A few complaints, sure. But a lot of kids don't care much for algebra, either; or slicing up a worm; or memorizing chemical formulae—but they survive.

192

The new menu might even spawn a generation of students who, as adults, will demand that Beaufort develop more eating places with sophisticated, international menus.

In deference to a few squeamish students, by the way, the tentacles are removed from the Fried Squid.

Osama...Who?

Like finding a needle in a haystack. Or a flea on a dog. Slippery, elusive Osama.

But we're determined to search for, capture, bring to trial and punish the al-Qaeda chief. Or seduce someone to rat on him, finger him, and be ready to exchange twenty-five million American dollars for Afghani...whatever their currency is.

"We'll hunt him down," promises our President, his jaw firmly and uncompromisingly set. "We'll dig through every pile of bat guano in every cave and tunnel to find him," swears Secretary Rumsfeld. "We'll re-landscape the Afghan terrain with a few more coyly named Daisy Cutters," promises Admiral Stufflebeem. And to the always sublimely confident Press Secretary Ari Fleischer, capture is a done deal.

Newspaper and TV reporters heighten the search drama with headlines like "Closing In," "Evidence Found," "Any Day Now," "Maybe Spotted."

The strategy of teeth-gnashing, chest-thumping, morale-pumping, and verbal heroics of the hunt may be exercises in futility. Osama is not going to appear conveniently on the stoop of a cave nibbling on dates, while waving a welcome at an approaching Personnel Carrier filled with U.S. Marines.

No. Our strategy of huff and puff, of solemn declarations of imminent triumph, of planning, plotting and bombing so that CNN cameras can record the parading around of a shackled Osama...all wrong.

It is unsubtle. It is expensive. But mostly, it leaves out a critical element: the ego thing. The more we hunt him down, the more his importance, cleverness and notoriety increase. We'll turn him into a holy icon, martyr, legend—a bigger-than-life hero, able to thumb a nose at both American and tribal chieftains. Able to move about with impunity, shadow-like, following secret trails his minions mapped out for him a long time ago.

No. No more chasing.

Declare officially, publicly and resolutely: Osama-baby, you're history. You're gone. A non-entity. Not worthy of the chase.

No more *ad nauseam* showing of film clips of Osama kneeling to fire a weapon, or quietly chortling over the ugly gig his boys pulled off on 9/11. (Don't bother to apply for an AFTRA card, Osama, after your mumbling TV spot.)

You're not important. You don't exist. No more dispatches, editorials, or political cartoons in the national press. You may have to publish your own newsletter, or get the Iraqi Bladder to run stuff on you.

Cave hop all you want—who cares? Shave off the beard, slip into some Hilfiger jeans, or get a nose job. Non-items.

We officially and formally blow you off as an irrelevant dustball.

You are politically neutered.

And you're certainly not worth 25 million. The 9/11 Fund can use it.

It may take a few weeks.

After that: Osama *who*?

Ode to a Creek

O K, so it's not the Bay of Fundy. It lacks the mystery of Loch Ness. There's none of the drama of the ocean's collision with the Maine coast.

There are no surfers challenging the great wave, no majestic schooners sailing proudly by, no pods of whales logging in the sun.

It's only Battery Creek, a sinuous, meandering offspring of the Atlantic that weaves its tentacled squiggly arms into the heart of the County. Dotted with islets of grass and oyster shells, the Creek has a unique and ever-changing landscape.

A shrimper in a small motorboat casting a net, a crabber pulling pots, or a pair of kayaks paddling the short sweep from US 21 to Battery Point is about all the water traffic the Creek can support. We follow their movements with binoculars, hoping they'll make it home before the Atlantic jealously sucks back its property.

For all its sprawling pattern, it's an intimate Creek—personal, on a people scale. It's a living, breathing organism. It inhales deeply to fill its channel with a refreshing swallow of seawater. And then, as the Moon commands, it reluctantly exhales, returning the water to Mother Atlantic.

And it has multiple personalities, endlessly shifting moods.

The Creek can be eerily still—so motionless that at times it looks like it died. But its glassy surface becomes an artist's canvas, capturing and reflecting the streaks of red, pink, mauve and orange strewn across its surface by both the rising and setting sun.

But let there be an ominous drop of the barometer, the Creek turns leaden and threatening. There's a molten heaving of the surface that seems to send a message: "stay off me. I'm getting angry."

And then the wind arrives, and the rain comes sheeting down; the Creek starts to churn and foam, toss and writhe itself into real waves and foaming whitecaps. No shrimpers or kayak paddlers now. Not the surly North Atlantic, to be sure. But a dramatic performance just the same.

Even in the pre-dawn hours, the Creek is not asleep. There is a strange luminescence that lends a soft glow to the water.

And when it's shrouded in fog, it has a spookiness that would rival any "Twilight Zone" episode.

At times, there's no Creek at all, just a wandering mud flat—as bleak and etched as the surface of the moon. The tide is out—way out—leaving behind a barren, gooey system of trickling streams. But not barren for long. The feeders arrive to indulge in nature's cafeteria: geese, blue heron, egret, pelican, and ibis appear to feast on little silver fish.

And when the weather is fair and the Creek is happily bloated with a fresh supply of ocean water, a pair of dolphins will gracefully glide by, performing their dive-and-surface choreography with remarkable grace.

It's not just a creek. It's our bond with the great Atlantic—and all the lands that lie beyond.

A Greek Gift

Two people are killed in a neighborhood shootout.
A tragedy.
Child dies trapped in well.
A tragedy.
Tenement fire kills family of six.
A tragedy.

Wrong. These are not tragedies, despite the way wire services, reporters, and news editors hype woeful events by using the word.

Please, for a few paragraphs, indulge a stuffy, pedantic, fussbudget ex-professor who still clings, pointlessly perhaps, to the original meaning of "tragedy."

Like so much else in Western culture, tragedy was an ancient Greek invention. The word itself translates as "goat song"—though it's baffling how this mundane definition connects with the high-minded, elegant, crushing forces that can bring down the mighty King Oedipus. Even the handful of scholars who can actually read and write classical Greek—a lush and sonorous language—haven't figured it out. Maybe an ancient playwright won a goat for turning out a great show.

A tragedy has to deal with a noble, heroic person embroiled in a morally significant struggle—a crisis that usually ends in ruinous defeat or death. To qualify as a tragic figure, you had to be a legendary hero, a great warrior, a powerful ruler. (Or a President?) But you're cursed with an affliction called a "tragic flaw," a gap in your moral armor—an excess of ego, pride or arrogance. It's a character disorder you may not be aware of or, maybe, choose to ignore.

And your downfall—inevitable, prophesied—will not only shake the nation, but serve as an ominous lesson on the fragility of power.

There's a reason why modern writers and editors should avoid the indiscriminate use of the ancient notion of tragedy. Tragic figures exist in the 20th Century who fit the classical definition. Two dramatic examples come easily to mind: Presidents Nixon and Clinton.

Both men were lofty figures, forceful leaders of "the most powerful nation on earth." Both, in their high office, wielded great authority and influence. Both felt they were immune to ordinary moral restrictions. Both occupied the prestigious Oval Office—the 20th Century equivalent of a Throne Room.

And both possessed a large dose of hubris—a character flaw, a tear in ethical fabric that blinded them to their faults.

Even as their terms of office started to wind down, neither Nixon nor Clinton fully grasped the corrosive nature of their hubris. Nixon: "I am not a crook." Clinton: "I did not have sexual relations with that woman."

It was not the FBI or Congress that did them in. It was the fierce and unforgiving Gods on Olympus that struck them down.

That's tragic.

What happened to the boy in the well, the victims of a fire, or the slain bystanders at a shootout is not tragic. It's certainly sad, melancholy, deeply pathetic, certainly heartbreaking. But it doesn't create a wrenching upheaval in the nation, the world, the universe.

Tragedy occurs only when greatness, nobility, and power self-destruct.

Talking to Plants

The list of things I do badly, clumsily, ineptly, sluggishly or indifferently would, if collected in book form, constitute a volume roughly the length of *The Oxford English Dictionary.* Or at least the *Lowcountry Phone Directory.*

It would make dreary reading.

My rate of failure in matters mathematical, mechanical, electrical, electro-mechanical, electronic, automotive, and astronomical is a figure slightly higher than my body temperature. (I've exaggerated my weakness about the heavens: I can, with calm conviction, identify the moon and sun.)

It's a male thing, I guess. No, it's really the helpless husband syndrome, a deficiency especially evident when a toilet overflows and my wife shouts "turn off the valve!" and I can't remember where the valve is. Or *what* it is.

But in one area of household responsibility, I'm peerless—an absolute giant among men, an unqualified master of competence and success.

Planting things.

As I stroll the aisles of a garden store, young unplanted flowers and shrubs, still fresh from mother nursery, call out: "Take me. Plant me. I trust you. I love you." Azaleas and caladium, Mexican heather and canna lily, dusty miller and dwarf camellia urge me to buy them. They know my secret.

When I plant a plant, I think like the plant.

I think: if I were this flower, still trapped in that plastic pot, impelled by a universal life force that demanded that I get securely rooted and flourish, what sort of loving treatment would I want?

So I dig the hole, carefully removing weed and tree roots, rocks, and hardened clumps of soil. The hole, of course, made wider and deeper than the root ball. The soil at the bottom of the hole is churned up, softened. The plant, in some shock, shouldn't exhaust itself trying to penetrate its roots into a new home.

Now I'll concoct the planting medium: one-third original dirt, one-third potting soil, one-third peat moss. ("The magic of peat moss!" a veteran gardener once told me.) With trusty watering can, I'll drench the mixture until it's soupy.

The plant is lowered in gently, and gently married to the mix. (I know, I know…those lateral roots are fragile!) The plant will issue a sigh as it merges with the welcoming soup. Before filling in around the root ball, the balance of original dirt will be mixed with a generous slug of peat moss (sphagnum peat moss, preferably), both to lighten the dirt and retain moisture.

When half filled, another dose of water to ease the crisis of entering a strange environment.

The plant needs to feel safe and secure. So the soil is pressed evenly and gently around the side of the ball, eliminating air pockets.

When the side filling is complete, I'll build a miniature wall of dirt around the base, turning it into a kind of retaining basin. When the plant gets watered again, the basin will hold it until it gently sinks in. The basin is now blanketed with peat moss.

Finally, mulch to cover the peat.

It's been said that plants will respond to gentle and encouraging words. So I'll conclude the planting ritual with: All set now? Comfortable? I pray you flourish and bring beauty to this garden.

It hears me.

My wife knows how to turn off the toilet valve.

The Joy of Writing

Back in June of 2001, I wrote a piece about finding ideas for a piece. An offer was made to *Gazette* readers: if there was a tumultuous demand (at least four requests) for a follow-up article on how a piece actually gets written, I'd happily oblige.

Well, it took only ten months for the four requests to trickle in. So as an honorable fellow, I offer herewith a brief depiction of the exhilarating ordeal of turning an idea into a 600 to 800-word essay.

A lot of things can trigger an article. A spoken word can do it. Or a memory, maybe. An innocent little news item buried on page six of a newspaper. A small fit of controlled lunacy, perhaps. A phrase of music. A passing anger, a jab of poignancy, a bite of melancholy.

Whatever the source, a seed gets imbedded in a few brain cells. It sticks, takes up lodging. I know it's there because it causes a certain restlessness, a psychic agitation that acts like a seductive lure dangling in front of a trout. I'm the trout.

Is it a subject worth exploring? Do I have the capacity and skill to handle it? Is there something worthwhile to put on paper? Does it have a "message?" (As a wit once observed: Got a message? Send a telegram.) Like a kid chasing butterflies, I swing a net trying to capture the ephemeral object—and miss. And miss again. The idea is a cocky imp, teasing then scooting away.

I have a fat file of scribbled, scrawled notes on ideas that misfired, that didn't ripen, that died aborning. Not ready. Not yet. Maybe later. Maybe never.

But a few ideas won't go away. Like a shrew, they nag, they pester, they start to obsess. I find myself jotting notes on napkins while out to dinner, on the back of grocery store receipts, along the edge of a bank deposit slip. The idea demands to be explored, tested, expanded. And it's beginning to control me.

But I've got to be careful. Maybe it's too soon to break out the yellow notepad and start scribbling. What if the idea is merely a flirtation, enticing but doomed to go nowhere.

I know I'm ready for the pad when, almost subconsciously, whole sentences begin to whistle through the brain. Are they an omen of a possible theme, a style, a tone? Might this primitive start lead to the creation of that mighty literary building block, a paragraph?

Now the engine of the brain begins to rev up, and I can no longer resist the siren call of a subject that insists on discovery, exposure, birth.

Writing can be a snarky, unpredictable business. Sometimes ideas and words rush onto the page like a lava flow that doesn't stop until the final period is attached to the final sentence. At other times, it's like pulling teeth, without the benefit of novocaine, grasping and straining for every word, phrase, sentence.

A random sentence or two begins to swell into a paragraph. No rational sequence of paragraphs yet. (Am I ever sure of what the finite, ultimate, exquisite order really is?) Never mind logic or structure at this point. I'll write it piecemeal, whatever part of the essay's body lures me first: the left foot is written; then the right shoulder; then a kneecap. With luck, the article's anatomy will be assembled into a coherent and readable piece.

When I type a first draft, I'm still editing and re-writing. I won't read this draft as it slides out of the printer. I'll let it "cook" for awhile—a few days, maybe a week or two. Then, with some trepidation, I read it again. My reaction is sometimes delight: Hey, that really hangs together. I said what I wanted to say. Sometimes, horror and revulsion is the reaction. The language is stilted, the theme is as clear as mud, the conclusion is so lame it needs a crutch. No reasonably sane editor would touch it. Back to work.

In an act of either desperation or abject surrender, the piece is done.

Done? Never. It is never done. Even after it's printed, I spot a dozen places where I should have used word x instead of word y; where I could have thinned and compressed better; where a transition was lame, almost decrepit.

So what? The act of writing keeps mold off the brain.

A Note on the Author

*A*nimals In My Mailbox is Joe Golden's seventh published book. The first six explored the triumphs and absurdities of cultural behavior in American communities.

He's written a dozen plays (many national prizewinners) for stage and television, and nearly two hundred articles and essays that appeared in professional journals in the U.S. and Canada. He was a faculty member at both Syracuse and Cornell Universities; hosted his own PBS television show for five years; was a member of a State Department delegation to study cultural changes in post-Mao China; and directed a study that led to the construction and operation of a three-theatre performing arts complex in Upstate New York.

And all the while he's both marveled and cringed at the behavior of those unpredictable bipeds called humans.

Joe and his wife, Lucy, moved to Beaufort in 1996 and found that the South makes a welcoming and wonderful home...even for Yankees.

Colophon

Tabby Manse ™

Coastal Villages Press is dedicated to helping
to preserve the timeless values of traditional
places along America's Atlantic coast—
building houses to endure through
the centuries; living in harmony
with the natural environment;
honoring history, culture,
family and friends—
and helping to
make
these
values
relevant
today.
This
book
was
completed on
April 15, 2003 at
Beaufort, South Carolina. It was
designed and set by George Graham Trask
in Times New Roman, a typeface created under the
direction of Stanley Morison for *The Times* in London in 1931,
with titles set in Comic Sans.